The Letters Of Tabula

Othniel Poole

Strategic Book Publishing and Rights Co.

Copyright © 2020 Othniel Poole. All rights reserved.

No part of this book may be reproduced or transmitted in any form or by any means, graphic, electronic, or mechanical, including photocopying, recording, taping, or by any information storage retrieval system, without the permission, in writing, of the publisher. For more information, send an email to support@sbpra.net, Attention: Subsidiary Rights.

Strategic Book Publishing and Rights Co., LLC
USA | Singapore
www.sbpra.net

For information about special discounts for bulk purchases, please contact Strategic Book Publishing and Rights Co., LLC. Special Sales, at bookorder@sbpra.net.

ISBN: 978-1-952269-23-3

Preface

Special thanks to Emily Humble for doing the front cover; really captures Tabula perfectly; and now I am more than accustomed to her face; Elohim bless you;

A Season of Whoops was a working title for some of the verse in this volume; sometimes lessons in life don't make sense as you are learning them. The Wisdom of this world is foolishness to God; and often Wisdom of the public is a glass of Jack Daniels and a game of darts.

Harold Bloom, the consummate literary critic took the influence of King Solomon and cried out on his cover "Where Can Wisdom Be Found?". According to Solomon, she cries aloud on the streets.

When one doesn't have a home, sometimes eating in secret is all you can do, because one is unseen. There is nothing delicious about hardship.

I once heard a Christian radio show about how the Japanese are very familiar with the idea of a father, and so the message of Christ seems reasonable, but there is the void of what it can actually contribute to their growing up. It was suggested that perhaps they need a mother figure.

We all have a mother; we have a father. Science investigates, and experimentation is some sense being the ultimate expression of Christian grace. Jesus was tried, hung on a tree and part of three on the trees, and he asks us to take up our tree and have a try and treating to the world good news.

People laugh at you when you have a try; they called Gohm and many dweebs and geeks in Australia "try hards"; but life is all about trying. We do; but how do you know what you want to do if you don't try? Little green men are defeated according to H.G. Wells. Gentle does it, there is no need for force.

It takes two to tango; it takes two to learn how to be in a Regatta. It takes two to enact the act and arrest of a criminal, the law and the sinner. It takes two to wed; and a third to administer the vows. Love is patient; love is kindness; life is kindred; life is family.

A memorable frankable: the Kingdom of God is a couple on the couch cuddled up with their kids watching Shrek. There are many in the world who do not even have enough to eat, and would love even two hours to feel safe and warm and well lit and well fed.

God bless the West? Let the West bless the rest!

Take it easy, live light, and may Jesus bless you; I hope you find something worth your time. Take that and nothing else;

Much love;

M. Othniel Poole

24th February 2020

Contents

Corporeal Breadbasket: 9
    Chapter 1: Coyworld 10
    Chapter 2: The Fishbowl Race 13
    Chapter 3: Memory Alliances 14

Allentown 2019 16
Fibre Baby 21
Respect Remedial B: 23
Kite Au Sol 24
King Ethelbert of Kent And The Temporal Catholic 25

MID LIFE EINSTEIN 32
    Chapter One: Playing Dice With The Universities 34
    Chapter 2: Love Is Like A Poem Full Of Weasel Words
    That Has Be We-Leased 41
    Chapter 3: Sentry To The Bell 43
    Chapter 4: Dreams Of Drinking And Waking Up Crying 45

That Book You Didn't Read 47
My Name is Birthday 51
Ballad Billy Londsdale 54
A Song For The Penultimate Generation 57
Kelly Is A Wakeup Call 63
I Wait For You 64

Amaxzing Blue Sue Chi And Edom Jakson The Cub 66
    Chapter One: Enezhi Nation 67
    Chapter 2: Posion. (With Exyra Whipped Soy Sauce) 69
    Chapter 3: Crew P 70

Chapter 4: The Sultans Of Grapes 71

Passion Of Luther Maundy 72
Passport Soon, Cuddles For Now 74
Cuckolopolis And The Orkney Androids 77
Ecce Leise Ace Says 80
Leonard Tulip And The Dimples 82
(Part Variable of Infinity) 88
Doctel Opel 90
Tenylee Bruce and Bruce Tenyeel 94
Pamela The Wise 95
Hidden Frustration 98
Captain Lion 100
Reykjavic Raga On Inferno Of Destinicore 101
Marrying An Anthrobram 103
HIDEOUS TORMENTS 105
My Punishment Is More Than I 106

Rosy Tot: 109
   1: Fragile, She's Dizzy 110
   2: Precious Wind, Seeds, Fruit, Sister 114
   3: Beset By Friends Met From Food 117
   4: Morning Dins (Anna And Redorthy) 122
   5: Weapons Of Nightmares 125
   6: Waiting For... And Something Unexpected 131
   7: Darcee's Nap 134

The Letters Of Tabula 136
   Bushranger Rosa's Love For His Daughter Toto Tabula 137

- Tabula To Daddy Rosa 139
- Deep Water In The Billy 141
- I'm So Glad I'm Not In Trouble 143
- Trust And Uber 145
- A Lullaby For The Bushranger 147
- Cool Oceans 150
- Jesser's Dresser 151
- Spill Derbins 152
- Green Days 153
- Rosebird 155

Darcee Gets An A+ 157
Sylvester Ryan Rosa Toby 177
The Gulf Of Neglect 181
Peace 182

Corporeal Breadbasket:

Struggles And Welcomes

17th-19th January 2020

1:11AM

Contents:

1: Coyworld

2: The Fishbowl Race

3: Memory Alliances

To Jaguar,

And Samantha Poole, my blood sister

Chapter 1:
Coyworld

17th January 2020

Lincoln Breadbasket was on the rosy estate that his family lived on.

He was at the pond, and it was full of coy carp.

"Hello coy of coyworld," said the General, and he tapped at the water, and it made ripples.

The coy just kept swimming around, making their turns, looking both ways in a world with no streets to dream on.

"I do like these spiffy fish," said Lincoln, "they need a holiday though, but they don't really act like they want one."

Saraph, Lincoln's sister, came over with a huge fishbowl.

"We're not going to play astronaut with this, okay, Linc?" she said, smiling, "we're going to get a fish, and you can take it on holiday somewhere on our property."

So the General scooped up a particularly mouthy fish.

"We are going to make you a public speaker," he said to the coy, "you can talk to all the birds and they will think you are amazing because they see you."

"They see you what, bro?" Saraph laughed.

"In a bowl," said Lincoln, "that's like a stadium!"

"But we're the only people watching the coy," said Saraph, "we see right through to her."

"How do you know it's a she?" asked her brother.

"Too much to explain right now, Linc," said Saraph softly.

She held his elbow and pointed in at the carp as it swum around in bowl.

"Isn't she beautiful?"

"I want to give her a cracker," said Lincoln, "I could just crush it up and feed it bit by bit; when it's all gone then it will be full. You only need one cracker."

"Yes," said Saraph, "I don't believe crackers is a state of mind you should give a fish. They get very angry if they're full up with something."

"I think you're like a cracker, sis," said Lincoln, "like a bon bon at Christmas, you're very sweet and kind and nice to me."

"What's a Saraph for; except for recording all the special details about her family?" she said.

Together, they walked through the parkland that was around their house.

There was a bridge and they went up and over it. It was made of sandstone and glue.

They found themselves at a clearing, and there was a man with long, long, long blonde hair and a prickly moustache.

"Hallo," said Lincoln, "I'm the Generally Breadbasket, and this is my fraternal guidance Saraph."

"Fraternal, that's a big word," said Saraph, "well done, Linc."

"I'm Benignus Bruhaha Moopy." said the man. "I like studying scarabs."

"Leave my sister alone," said the General.

Saraph grabbed her brother's arm.

"Don't fight, General," she said, "that's more insulting to me than if you just left it."

Benignus produced a square plastic box with holes across the top.

"Look inside, Generally." said Benignus, and pointed.

And inside was a scarab that was blue with azure glittery bits. It had shiny green eyes like Christmas, and a kind smile, and little teeth like antlers on a gazelle.

"Does it have a name?" whispered the General.

"I call it Botolph Baseball," said Benignus.

Chapter 2

The Fishbowl Race

17th January 2020

The General and Benignus had their containers for their pets, and Saraph had the starting gun at the arch of a long, athletically decorated gravel path.

"Okay, boys," she said, laughing, "we're going to have a race."

"Let's see who's better?" said the General, "A bon bon fish or a doob doob beetle."

And Saraph held one ear, her left ear, with her finger and scrunched her eyes real tight, then held the flare gun as high as she could and fired.

BWANG!

Benignus started running with his scarab in his case. The General, standing just where he was, lobbed his fishbowl like a discus, and it went tearing through the atmosphere to the finish line, which was a drinking well filled to overflowing. It was really more like a very deep spa, and was very good for swimming.

"Come on fishy!" cheered the General.

The fish fell out of the bowl, and went over some unfamiliar places in the pool, swimming happily.

"It's happier than a pig in mud," said the General, "and we win!"

Benignus stopped running.

"I can't throw a race," he said, "can you let me finish?"

"Finish him!" said the General, and Saraph fired the flare a second time.

So Benignus ran and ran and ran and ran and ran.

Chapter 3:
Memory Alliances

19th January 2020

While they were waiting for Benignus to return, Saraph and General Breadbasket went into the living room of their house and opened their Bibles.

"We're going to learn some memory verses," Saraph said, "together, okay. As a team."

"No, it's not good to compete," said the General, "why is a brother born for rivalry though?"

"No, it doesn't mean to fight, silly; it's when someone's fighting you and your brother helps."

"Fight the good fight," said the General, "and he who finds a wife finds a good thing. But it is not good to fight your wife. That is a bad fight."

"If your eye is good, your whole body is filled with light."

"You can see inside me, God?" asked the General.

"He has searched you and known you, he knows when you sit down on this couch and when you rise to play in the park."

"Does he have a phone book to search me?"

"Well, he has a book of life, and your name is there, Lincoln. And a name that God gives you that no one knows."

"I bet it's Matthew,"

"What?"

"Nevermind."

"Love the Lord your God with all your heart, soul, strength and mind."

"Is love a feeling or a doing?"

"General," said Saraph, "you care for people."

"So I care with my heart," said General, pointing to his chest, "I can care for people. I can go hunting with them, and I can eat their food when they make it for me. And I can talk to the stranger and the sojourner."

"Sojourner!" said Saraph. "That's very good General, another big word for you."

"I can care with my soul too," said the General, "I can walk many miles until my shoes never wear out. That's how it works, right?"

"But you're not aimless," said Saraph, "you've got a promised land to go to."

"Where is it, Sar?"

"Somewhere out window," said his sister, "somewhere in the open, somewhere."

"There's a place for us," said General.

"Very saintly thoughts," said Saraph.

Allentown 2019

28th December 2019
1:00AM

Egypt was around, and the tourists
Listened to the socio florists
Moab dandled crow dust da
And Jesus spoke a word to me
"It is for freedom that I set you free."

Lamech brutalised the corn
And Edom flipped a will to stitch
And Jesus called the woman on
And said "drink deep and bring your son."

Depression, here I warn you
You do not want the sushi hand
See if you can understand
"If you love me, obey my command."

When two sides both want your heart
And they try to work you out
Remember the Son of Man
"I know the hope and future plans."

When two sides want submission
And you are scripting all your moves

Remember the artist of Love
"Oh for the wings of dove."

When two sides promise advance
While you dance round in underpants
You wished the two could become one
In these tests, God lends some friends
And then you'll get the dividends
And then you'll make all the amends
And reparations
From Essendon, Albion Station
And Harvest Bible College too
And all the places where you wept
Cabrini sheets white starched
On which you gathered
As the Father
Between lines
Administered the cryptic beef and wine

The just shall live by faith
And mercy is a part of this
To be excused is a relief
And that often creates a seed

But when the Sour wants destroy
He'll take the excuse from the boy
And all you have is an account
Of an unbalanced amount

Othniel Poole

And then you admit you were wrong
And then people think they can lead
And they instruct you for your bread
And they want mysteries of wed
And so do I, and I would love
To name the feathers of the dove
And call to God from up above
As Father, brother, prince and king
And go no further than a tingling
It's easy when there's counterpoint
The women in this Franga joint
Sing dirges in a merry chain
As Taylor Swift rides on a plane

Mock on, mockers, call men names
I have had it everywhere
And then behind your hands whisper
And I would like a hand to hold
Do you love your ways so much
That you would be to me so cold?

Two bows aimed right at my teeth
And if I obey, one release
And if I try and solve this math
They might call me a tetripath

I would like to see them with balloons
Yelling, surprise and let me in
To finally walk through that door

And I won't be alone no more

Yes, it may be vintage kris
And the scar is less than this
I believe in outer space
For that is heaven's icon place

And I could sail Andromeda
I'm still to understand the craft
And we could see with cor de sight
And be so glowing, free from fright

Much religion leaves the mites
Out in places with Mortein
And a man needs to speed
At seventy and five
Because a man can't live on
Just a quarter stein

Much spirituality
Without spittle and snot and keratin
Is not the kind I want to have
I want a full and bustling mind
Pretty much all of the time

For real bodies are the thing
And archiving yesterday
There is no now, just later and before
The city, not construction site

Othniel Poole

    And the ancient British moor

      If all could see
      If all could

       1:17AM

Fibre Baby

**14th February 2020
4:44AM**

Hand resting. Open.
No origami with fingers
Let's rock with the inmates
Of Alcatraz
Raspberry Tigers pray for me
Sweet seraphs
I am so happy they are happy
I love them so
And I don't need a plastic phone
To know of who is True
Much love
Women absolutely can have it all
And that is wisdom you can frame
In the Holy of Holies
I like being kaspian
I like being my genotype
And I don't need
Witness relocation in the shady sense
To be redeemed
But I am seeking a house
And I love to be lived
May the Branch bless you
With Fruit that you bought

Othniel Poole

                    From Vinnie's
                 They do new stuff
                As well as the old
             That's what a novel means

Respect Remedial B:

17th February 2020

Frankston says do not relapse
Have respect not hat and greet attacks
Babel cigarettes and wet attempts to read
I am sorry, Aussie blokes are salt and earth
Of globe, and St Anne says that's light
Dana Barrett and me love the screen
Here is an immaculate fancy
I love my Mum. And I love a Kirk
Keep my safe in Osment begging
I respect the Aussie bloke.
I repent
But do not forget the words I said
Do not forget Quan Yeoman's Red
So we do what a best Jean said
As David trembles in Abishag's bed
Kesteeoolll and wease

Kite Au Sol

27th January 2020
9:49AM

As she walked through the cosmos;
Kite was free to be who she was;
And loved loved loved grew loving;
And laughter echoed in her chest;
And as the gold from mead so veil;
The sun in sky turned honey pale;
And as a mink turned in her skin;
The sun let spirit come on it;
And let us see the ghost upon the sol;
And let us see the grief upon the temp;
And let us ease the honey from the jar;
And let us lay aside our ebony and mustard
Air guiter;

King Ethelbert of Kent And The Temporal Catholic

13th January 2020

Special Thanks To Samuel Cardwell; who was the first to read this.

King Ethelbert of Kent (560-616AD) was the first British English monarch to convert to Christianity. His wife was Bertha, princess of Paris, who was a Christian first and had her own vicar from France named Luiudhard.

He was made a saint by the church in future years, but it all didn't run smoothly to begin with...

"Ah Bertha, fair sweet thing that smiles like moon that hasn't full balloon

And bear to me what you will, and what is thusthis? A trust?

That your vicar says for me to forgo lust?

Of course, that I will and still I be with you.

Because to love me is your point of view.

And into my laws, I will protect your kin;,

I will let every vicar, bishop in;,

I will let them convict every peasant,

Every duke and every duchess,

Every undercover harlot of their sin.

And what? For what? That thy thou edify,

That thy thou listen to thy countenance,.

That face of your proverb dancing on my ears.,

Yet, there are some among these,.

Men of kingdom not of mine - ,

And that that they are not of my kingdom,

But are under my taxes,

Is no business of mine.

As you have taught me, sweet Betty,.

That I need eyes to see;,

But when they do miraculous,

I must admit it FRIGHTENS me!

Away, I say, you cordians!

You blue risk of mortgage pylon adamantine subsifitch,

And yet you hold mye hand,

And I am healed of this amount,

Not as much as your King Saul.

From your Old Testament he be,

That, so tormented,

Put on tunes,

By a singer very small,

And very simple very ruddy,

Very festive, close as kin;

As Jonathan sheds down to skin,

And gives his armour over,

Oh, that would an heir apparent,

Make the king's daughter a parent,

But that would take a miracle

He would have to turn,

From his disgust,

And trust that they could get along;,

And he'd no need to look across the balcony,

Into the bath of purgatory,

And all the white devil bureaucracy.

And hark, sweet Betty, you just sit:

The Letters of Tabula

As revival spreads within my duchy of Kent.
You say that Augustine,
Not our British patron,
But the one of Hippo's height,
When Roman Empire drew to night,
That there were signs and wonders,
Bringing broken citizens,
Whose papers now meant nothing:
Small as Paul in dictionary
Feeling bitter, feeling scary
That these signs and wonders
More than all Augie's long treatise.
Of the City of the Lord.
That these touches close of God
Would heal a broken heart,
That there had been a death of art,
And all the saint's statues
Those redeemed busts and blues
Would not matter anymore;
For as Nokter the Stammerer
Has burbled in biography:
The Holy Roman Empire
Was coming;
But I do not feel rich,
Even though I am a king,
I do not want to die by holy breath,.
My doubt and confusion,
Makes me think of other times."
And Bertha rested with the King,

And held his hand another time,
As the Holy Spirit,
Dressed as a hiker of Emmaus,
Subtle and so soft,.
Without words and with the holy conduct,
Would be enough for Ethelbert to submit,
And call the God of Abraham his Master.
"You know, o Eth! That Gregory the Great
That Pope of Church, aspiring state,:
He Ccondemns me because I have not won you to my Lord;.
(And Salic laws of Clovis may be in your views the noblest -.
I do not speak so well of all your declarations).
And that I be so frank -. tThat I be on your town and in your team -.
And you not speak cessation.
You know these things are real.
And your old ways are like the wineskin;
And you are not merry, dear.
Come, and see, your citizens
They all embrace the Nazarene.
Do you see their changed lives?
Just where they've been?
And I know he can change your heart;
And you won't be afraid of what
You do not understand.
With that legislative head of yours,
And you will receive he'vn's heav'n's applause -,
Not that it is by your mer't,
But by the Holy Spirit.
Oh watchword, deep. Thus, I say:

Despite your soulish disarray,!
Come to my order from your decay!"
And Ethelbert he cast his crown
Within his mind and wrote another precept down.
He allowed the monasteries,
Benedict and sanctuaries.
"All for peace, that is well good.
But sometimes supernatural
Is such a blistering alarm.
Why would a God that would forgive
That e'en to your Moses,
Would Ddo HIM harm?"
And Bertha rested quietly;
She was at rest;
She had entered
The promised land.
It was a Kent
That wasn't common, crude or spent;
That wasn't anything but peace and light.
It wasn't a monopoly;
It wasn't an old road that led,:
As Bunyan said, to Destruction;,
It wasn't a place where a pilgrim,
When he saw the tongues of fire:
Put his fingers in his ears,
And blasphemed the beloved
For way far too many years.
"Oh Jesus, Bertha, forgive me.
I am but a little boy.

Give me dreams and wonder once more;
Let me enter into joy."
And Ethelbert he wept so soft;
With hardened features pearling up.
And Liudhard took the holy water,
And made a saint-husband,
For that Parisian's sweet daughter.

Mid-Life Einstein
8th - 9th January 2020
5:06PM
To Amanda and Joseph Keck
You have been through a lot
And it is by God's genius
That you are through it

A man is in the bathroom with two boxes of silver hair dye, the contents comes out dark like leeches, and he sticks in on his sticky out hair, which to begin with is brown like mousse de chocolat.

He has a towel over his shoulder, tan and pale, and though he is in midlife, he still has acne across his chest.

He nudges at his red moustache with his two middle fingers and smiles.

He rinses his hair and it comes out silver, just like the box.

MID LIFE EINSTEIN

CONTENTS:

1: Playing Dice With The Universities

2: Love Is Like A Poem Full Of Weasel Words That Has Be We-Leased

3: Sentry To The Bell

4: Dreams Of Drinking And Waking Up Crying

Chapter One

Playing Dice With The Universities

8th January 2020

Our silver haired friend walks into the local bar with two oversized rubiks cubes in his left hand. People are on pokie machines and watching the TAB.

A horse will win the Melbourne Cup for sure, he thinks.

He walks up to the bartender and speaks:

"I bet your bottom dollar I can answer any question you have to ask me."

"Oh yeah, mate?" says the bartender, surly, sweaty, unshaved, in a singlet that looks like a used hankie.

"I bet you can't even pronounce your name," says a man in a flamingo jacket, leaning against the bar, very skinny, with sunglasses with yellow rims resting on top of his shaved ginger head.

"I Am Yahu," says the man with the silver sticky out hair, and shaking the Flamingo's hand, "way cool name, I reckon. But you can call me Albert."

"Did you come to get drunk?" says a lady in crimson, very little crimson and with straps as narrow as lone fibres of rhubarb. She's leaning on the bar also, to the left of our hero.

Flamingo rolls his eyes and looks through a deck of cards in his right hand, half of them are business cards, half of them are the best winning cards for Blackjack.

"Well, we are water, mostly," said Albert, his voice going up a notch in a squeak, "if you had a hygenic process, perhaps you could healthily drink from a human being. I don't think it is been mastered yet, or would be very marketable. But it is best to drink from a cup."

"A cup..." said the Crimson Lady, as if in epiphany, "of course. And here I am drinking from schooners."

"A schooner is a skimming stone," said Albert, "it's also a sailboat. But I prefer Pacers, myself."

"Alcohol, brother," says Flamingo, "she wants to know if you are drinking tonight. What's your poison?"

"Well, I don't believe that God plays dice with the universe," said Albert, "that's my fear. Sometimes fear is crippling. Sometimes fear can stop you doing what you love. It makes bad what is good, and is a cage for the soul. So I guess you could say that Fear is my poison."

The Crimson lady giggles.

"So I've got to face my fears, and so I came here, to the Taberet."

"Get this man an apple cider," said Flamingo, banging his left hand flat on the bar.

"Settle down," said the bartender, and gets a Strongbow for Albert, "you ever drank cider before, Albert?"

"That be blasphemy," said Albert, "in the sense that it's appleing, and also incomprehensible mathematics. But love trumps mathematics."

"Don't tell the gamblers that," said the bartender.

"What's your name anyway?" Yahu asked the Crimson Lady.

"Tamar," she said, offering a limp, manicured hand, "Elizabeth S. Tamar."

"You sure you don't want a beer, mate?" the bartender said, as Yahu took the cider.

"I'm very wary of yeast," said Albert.

"Many wise men come from the yeast," says the bartender.

"That's also blasphemy," said Albert, "you may as well say that babies come from the stork."

"And you have said it by quoting it," said Flamingo.

"Quoting isn't believing," said Albert, "memorisation isn't consent."

"I'll remember that," said Flamingo, "stay away from me, you storker."

"So I bet you can't answer this question, Albert," said Tamar, "Can you tell me about your love life?"

Albert scratched his silver head.

"Can you give me a coin?"

"But you haven't won the bet," Tamar whined.

She crumpled over as she said it, then regained her composure.

She handed over a coin.

"What is this on it?" said Albert, pointing to one side.

It was a pair of lips.

"A kiss," said Tamar.

"Well," said Yahu, "give to kisses what is due kisses and to God what is due God's."

Yahu looked at the cider, opened but untouched, bottle cap on the bar. He grimaced and left it there, walking out.

"Hey, that cost a lot of money, brother," called Flamingo.

"I'll bet it did," said Albert.

"Aw..." said Tamar, "look me up on Facey, Albert!"

"That's generally what polite eyes do," said Albert, "God bless you, Miss Tamar."

Albert walked from the bar down the street.

"Hi Albert," said a boy in a tuxedo, running up to him as he walked, "I'm going to my uncle's wedding today. It's going to be so much fun. There's going to be marshmallows, and I reckon I can store about five of them up my nose."

"Dimensional extras," said Albert, "I shall not crave those delicacies, keep me from the snares that they have laid for me. And let the wicked fall into their own nets."

"Are you speaking about the darkweb, Albert," said a little girl, who had also caught up with them. She was wearing a blue and white tartan bonnet, like the top of a jar of homemade market jam.

"There is dark matter, that's what's the matter," said Albert, "some say it is lovely, but they have not interpreted what they have not read. They condemn without a fair view, they criticise on the fact that it has been criticised, and so others criticise on the recommendation of their criticism. This is a critcal issue."

"Sounds like a big issue," said the boy, "do you have a place to stay tonight, Albert?"

"The imagination of man's heart is evil from his youth," said Albert, "who would write the story of my life the way that it has been?"

Sorry, Albert, but it does get better.

I bet you it does.

And even if you lose, I'll make you very rich and heaven sent in the end.

"Thanks mate," said Albert to me, somewhere in the air, somewhere in his face. Somewhere out there.

Then he faced the boy, the three of them still walking.

"I have a bathroom I've been sleeping in," said Albert, "I was able to dye my hair tonight. A grey head is the crown of glory. Amazing greys, how sweet the sound. Perhaps I can put them on my violin bow."

"Just don't dress up and ride a white horse," said the girl.

"White, pale," said Albert, "it's all shady when you can't discern, or you do not know why you hold a prejudice."

"I've been reading Jane Austen," said the boy.

"Watch it doesn't crush you," said Albert.

"Albert," said the girl, "you could come stay with us."

"And who is us?" said Albert.

"We're just across the pond," said the girl, "we live in a little house... back of the bush."

"And who are your parents, sweetheart?"

"Judith and Barry Pariah," said the girl, "and my name is Amanda."

"Amanda Pariah," said Albert, "pleased to meet you. I will come to your family's house, for certain I will, but I will sleep outside."

"Oh, that's no problem, Albert," said Amanda, "we are very used to outsiders, we Pariahs."

"And my name is Eustace Cahn." said the boy.

Albert produced a mandarin from his jacket and threw it to the boy.

"Always good to have a snack," Albert said.

"What are you going to eat, Albert?" asked Amanda. "I'm worried about you. You can't just give away everything."

"I haven't given away my dice," said Albert, motioning to his two oversized rubik's cubes.

"You haven't even started figuring them out," said Eustace.

Eustace then was busy unpeeling the mandarin.

"That's not the main course," said Albert, "man can not live on mandarin alone, but on every word that comes from God, and that's in Hebrew. You might like to have that fruit with kombucha, that's a brew he likes."

"Fungus juice," muttered Eustace.

"Don't bag it," said Albert, "it's not good, it's no good, then off he goes and boasts about his purchase."

"Then cut to the purchase," said Amanda, "can I have some kombucha, Albert?"

"We'll have to go to the milk bar," said Albert, "before we go to your house, the house of the Pariahs."

And there just happened to be one on the way, and they all went in.

There was a man who looked more like a portly chef crossed with a butcher than a milk bar owner. But who are we to expect what we expect?

"I'm expecting they'll have kombucha here, sir," said Albert to the milk bar owner.

"We have a lot of chocolate," said the owner, "but yes, we do have kombucha."

"Do you have chocolate kombucha?" asked Eustace.

"You should invent that," said the milk bar owner, "I wouldn't know the mix."

Albert picked two honeycomb kombuchas for Amanda and Eustace, and he picked a grape and milk one for himself.

"Grape and milk?" grimaced Eustace.

"It's good for the eyes," said Albert, saluting to his temple.

They all got straws made out of real straw, and went down a side street sipping away.

"The nearer your destination, the more you need a refill of your kombucha," said Eustace.

"Destination honeycomb," said Amanda, "bom, bom, bom, bom... bom."

"Accusation nation," said Albert, "polite-icks, righteousness by faith and wraiths writing diesel on the back of the wandering stars, destined for a long poem in a letter against a post-Eustace world. Heaven preserve you, Eustace Cahn."

"And don't become a postman," said Amanda, "deliver us from deliveries."

Amanda put a hand in the air, a single finger pointed to heaven.

"For thine is the..." said Amanda.

"Oh, we're here," said Eustace.

And so they were, a corrugated iron house, like something out of Storm Boy, but with three stories.

Chapter 2

Love Is Like A Poem Full Of Weasel Words That Has Be We-Leased

8th-9th January 2020

And as he slept outside the Pariah's house, Albert sang this song to himself. He played the gumleaf between two right hand fingers, and the washboard with his left foot. He also wore a hat that looked like a popcorn box, with the red and white stripes and "Pop" written in big bold black.

Would that I be a rose

Would that I be a rose in a dungeon

Would that I be a rose in a black weed dungeon of schools

Would that I be a rose in a garden of unexpected

Would that I be righteousness in a field of daisies

Would that I be destiny and truth to the little ones

Would that I be honour and establishment and holy writ

And so what is?

Why do you list the reasons of your mind, and so I wonder

So love, so love

And that is what you demonstrate

And fear can be merely

That you don't know what is going to happen next

But God does

And the rememberance of that

Othniel Poole

Sense that

What is here

So reap, Albert. Reap your notes.

Chapter 3

Sentry To The Bell

9th January 2020

Albert woke up in the morning before the Pariah's had woken up.

Judith Pariah was sitting on the verandah, her mouth wide open and the flies dancing lazily around in very Oodnadatta elipses. She had thick grey hair like the top of a squeezed toothpaste tube. And she was comfortably cuddly and wore a full dress like teatowels in autumn.

Barry Pariah was bailed out on a long bamboo recliner with white pillows as grubby as the bartenders singlet. Maybe one or two more grass stains, and a few open holes baring sponge coloured foam. He was big and beer like and bear like and bear of arms, though his arms, though bared were hairy like a bear. His head was hairy, if you were judging how arms were hairy, but for a head of hair, it was yet to return to full vigour.

All will be made right at the Resurrection of the Dead.

"Hi Albert," said Amanda Pariah, jumping down from the verandah. "What are you up to today?"

"I've got these cards from your Mum last night," said Albert, showing Amanda a deck of cards, "when you're in business, when you're a scientist and an entrepreneur and a pokies stock broker like I am, you need business cards."

"But these are none of your business," said Amanda, "silly, they're my mum's!"

"And she gave them to me," said Albert, "and Barry doesn't like gambling anymore, he's born again. You shall have to get him some

Baby Likes Brahms on your live stream, I think. That's what born again people like, right?"

"But Albert," said Amanda, "How do the cards help you? How are they going to help people find where you are?"

"Well," said Albert, "I have a theory. It is the theory of language. I call it the theory of punitive justice."

"Do you want to be a judge, Albert?"

"No, Amanda," said Albert, bobbing down onto his knees and looking her in the eye.

He produced a card, it was the King of Diamonds.

"See, this is my card. My reference to you," he said, very softly in the dawn, "I could speak empty words, I could speak swelling words. But this speaks 1000 words, because it is a picture."

"But how do I *find* you again, Albert?" Amanda whined.

"Well, you take that card, Amanda," said Albert, handing it to her, "and being a card you shall find me in the shuffle."

"I don't like tap dancing," Amanda huffed.

Albert began to walk away into the rising sun.

"We are all water, mostly," said Albert, "tap into your live stream and you'll find me in the shuffle. And then you can dance with me, if you want to dance with me."

Amanda smiled as Albert grew further away from the Pariah's house.

"Goodbye Albert," said Amanda, waving with one hand and securing her bonnet with the other.

Chapter 4

Dreams Of Drinking And Waking Up Crying

9th January 2020

Albert found himself by a waterfall and a dam, surrounded by long grass. It was the kind of grass that is almost like wheat, and nothing like darnel.

It takes an expert in cereals to know the difference.

In this episode, Albert took a piece of grass and made a fishing rod from it.

"In this part of the world, there are yabbies," said Albert, "there are bound to be yabbies, and where there are yabbies, there are yabby stories, and yabby abbeys with yabby archbishops and stained yabby windows."

The dam had a bit of froth on top, mud and this and that.

"That's definitely a stained window," said Albert, "and I can see my face in it."

He took one of his rubiks cubes and looked at the reflection of himself with it.

"A reflection tells me that I need to fix the puzzle," said Albert, "it shows me from another way how to fix the puzzle. But it doesn't fix the puzzle, it just shows me I have a puzzle. And it obscures the yabbies deep inside. And I really want to hear one of those yabby stories."

He threw his rubiks cube in the dam. It floated on top like a cork.

"That's curious," said Albert, "once you pass through reflection, you no longer relflect on what has passed, but some things still remain to be reflected on."

The cube began sorting through its patterns by itself, there bobbing around in the dam.

Albert widened his eyes and gaped with his mouth, totally self sacrificing his dignity.

"I hope there isn't a rational explanation for this," he said, softly, "that would be *so* disappointing."

He walked over the dam, on the water's surface, without sinking, picked up the cube and walked back.

It was complete and solved.

That Book You Didn't Read

12th January 2020

Somewhere, people are saying new words;
And some new words are often what you need.
Even old words may be new,
As Webster is quite tall.
The dictionary's reputation
Surpasses the TV;
And the Bible is full of words
The holiest you'll ever find;
And even those
Genealogies that go so long;
For I believe
God's Family will renew mind.

And that old man he is not you;
He's just pulp fiction feed.
He's just that paper villain
In that book you didn't read.

And all old shame is not your name
And all old ice is broken.
By that "Busted!" burning heat
When God has spoken.

And when the squatter's in your house

Othniel Poole

Because you did not shut up shop.
Just hold the white stone in your dreams,
And know what alabaster means.

See your friends for who they are
And not for their fridge doors;
For real food is what is important
Not the indecisive pause.

See your leaders with great hope;
For didn't they hand you a rope?
And remember to spell good news
The right way and do not display
Confusion, randomness, decay.

I knew a certain man
Who lived surrounded by
Massive ventriloquist dummies.
He had trouble communicating!
Phonies are not smart,
And faux it isn't friend.

I knew a certain face to face
That was like the human race;
How can you go fish for men
When on the line all men debate?

I knew a holy son of light,
And I looked into the soul,

And I for while would take me time,
And ponder this:
A normal electricity.

I knew the squint of understanding,
Scrutiny can be demanding,
It is not a plague of locusts,
As true colours they come into focus,

I knew the weeping of the heart,
And I knew just where to start,
But when the quill is held by Lord,
You should do as you're told.

I knew the context continued,
We aren't a malfunction'ng PC.
But as we've sown, so it has grown,
And what you loved now returns the sympathy.

I knew ambitions of the young,
For you the solar system hung.
And you have dreams
Like I had;
But you have a different pontifex.

I knew the red tape through the bus;
And Jane Eastern's a back reference;
A chiropractor's in sci-fi conventions;
Making cracks and breaking all the tension.

Othniel Poole

And our hand,
The back of our hand,
Is nothing like a psych ward.

And our hand,
The back of our hand,
Is nothing like trouble.

And our hand,
The back of our hand,
Is nothing like cultic.

And to us our hand is noun?
And to us our hand is verb?
And to us our hand is reaching
For the lamb where once was proffered herb

"But the righteous man holds to his way, and the one with clean hands grows stronger." - Job 17:9

My Name is Birthday

26th January 2020

Hello friends, I am foraging through teeth like mountains;
They rise from the plain of the black woods of gorse;
My name is Birthday; and the amourous horse;
That I wore on my lapel; you knew her well;
And I love you so; more than you know;
My name is Birthday; I'm giving you Creedence;
I'm giving you days to enjoy ones deferrence;
I'm giving you joy and I'm giving you wings;
I'm giving you all kinds of springs;
Set me alight; oh how you burn bright;
Set me on heat; There is warmth in my seat;
Set me so free;
Lord God Almighty; how you are Wise;
I do not think myself haughty in my eyes;
For the salt of the Earth doesn't come from decay;
Let all the Fred Hollows heal and unravel;
Father, you rule so well and so true;
Let me be so true to you and to you;
Let me be Father of many inside;
The tombs where Lazarus left a Birthday inside
My name is Otto;
I'm humble and foolish;
My tummy is big; And my ears are to speak;
And my righteousness grows;

Othniel Poole

And the Lord God will show;
And God is a dealer; a healer; a bringer of recipocity;
And I love you sol; more than you crawl;
And I love your pspeach; more than u reachl;
Ad I grace your flaws; more than you jaws;
And I give you hand; more than we jammed in the sand;
I love you face; I love you neck; I love you Jesu; I love you when
I love you so when you approach and sow; I love you when you make kosher the ken;
I love when barbecues are made of gems;
I love you again and gaina and gaina;
We see this as a; no listen, door soil catcher;
We need to do this for a while;
So smile and let us discuss or pus;
And then we will catch a great business car;
And then we will no show oscar;
As my head is filled with dread;
I know on the surface that I'm like the one
That you want to wed, and we will; oh my so!
As you read mu words; let me tell you, my bau;
I love you now; and I love your meow;
I love you powe and I love Lord Howe;
I love your methods and I love your records;
I love your destiny; I love your speace;
I love your friends and I love every grace;
I love your dearness your nearness to me;
Let us wend our way through the dawn of the kwy;
And let me be good to you; holy good sol;
And let me love you oa awesoe deco;

And let me enhoy and ease up on the ro;
And let me de si on the bi oa o 2;
Breathe in beau, breathe in the good hair;
Breath in my face and make me taste ace;
And male me a litter and form me a word;
And let me be u and let u be so id
Love is a good thing; and Yersua oft;
The one who desecneds from the nole in the loft;
And the one who makes letters so noble and wise;
Wbaat can we se. Sleah

Ballad Billy Londsdale

Bunurong Champion
26th January 2020

Let me speak of my land:
The land where I, hey;
I was increasing in steps;
And I have made many new friends.
My name, according to you, you sirs:
Is Billy Londsdale!
And while you're breaking fists;
And offering your peace at dawn;
When our engagement grace was born;
And while you're eating dessert;
I can insert this insert:
And tell you of my life,
Across the sand and sea and sky.
I go with my friends: laughing time many;
And you laugh at my name?
You laugh my name in overtures:
And in my author's eyes
I am Classic.
As I run like David's son?
As I run across my land?
As I give my brothers a hand?
My fellers are going so well;
And my friend Thomas;

Who is just like us;
And yet he is so different;
Offers us Divine Service.
We understand his heart,
For his Ruach Hakodesh;
He meets us in the midst of things;
And we know better than he,
How to the Spirit sing.
This may be Doctor Livingstone to you;
But this is no place for Elephants;
Not in Coolurt or anywhere.
Across the Protectorate of Bunurong;
You may say, "this man is sick!
He is so very eager, and enthused,
And you may say, "his heel is bruised,"
But you know I am a character;
That you cannot forget once met;
Even though in future,
Many white feller,
Who live here,
Has not checked.
Please, sir, let us have some room;
And let us not bind kinder things to soon;
For bitter things are not our gratitude.
It was not our intention!
It was our lack of food;
And your London has lined us not!
We do not want your kind of drink!
If you will not feed our heads;

Othniel Poole

We'd rather go without your clothes;
That you hand us within your schools.
Our tree is more than something pale,
We both say that towards;
One to one and mouth to mouth;
Oh, bring us back to life;
Pray law informs us of enough of both our swords!
And I am more than impulse, lion!
We'd rather meleleuca tree,
And to see the love we want,
Than your frank English Rose,
And always kept upon your toes!
Clay by water is no irony;
Let's acknowledge everyone's dirt
And then go out to sea;
To see what's cooking this double 13;
It is rather average, if I may say;
To be so mean;
We are not German, English, French;
And you are not the ubermensch;
We are Bunurong.
And this is a way of coping,
And similiar to facts,
Like Gabriel singing in reverse:
We remember a song!

A Song For The Penultimate Generation

28th September 2019

We don't need to experiment in uni
Unless it's something like playing with fingerpaint
Or pushing our toy truck through the sand
Or making dough, getting it baked and sharing the
Bread with our friends

The cafe at uni is out of tomato sauce
But they're a consensus there
They'd rather have smashed avo
Poor avocado

Johnny is the boss of the cafe
She has a goldfish in a bowl
There used to be two
But someone wished they were
Somewhere else
And that fishy
Took the wish seriously

She makes cupcakes with pink icing
And ballbearings that are edible
Yes, university is the place of innovation
We watch the news

Othniel Poole

And someone powerful on the air
Makes sure there's no good news
Why is that, Johnny?

I talk to Johnny for six days
And on the seventh day
We take a trip into the city
She takes my directions
And I follow the lines of the map

We arrive at a courtyard of alabaster
And it smells of nard and parchment
Someone is suing two men
For gazing in view of a woman
Who was trying to get clean

They said another man was with her
And they wanted to report it
But it was them, with their CCTV
That needed reporting
This was the first case of the judge
That day
God as my witness

Me and Johnny stayed for half an hour
In silence
And then we went to the fairy floss shop
And she bought a beautiful red handbag
She had to go to the bathroom

And I held it for her as I watched the X-Files
On a demo TV at JB HI Fi

I don't remember seeing this episode
It was about two men who broke an alien
In two and ate her over cheese and onion chips
It was terrifying and I wanted to jump in the handbag
Like a Jack Russell dog
And hide

Johnny returned and she had tied a ribbon in her hair
It was aquamarine and quite beautiful
She looked like an American Fundamentalist Evangelical now
Whatever that means

"Do you like the movies?" she asked me with a smile of small teeth
like a director, and I said:
"Only if they're not promoting compromise."
"Oh, a Keith Green, fan," she laughed, and started singing
"Sheep and the Goats."

Then we went to a vegan protest. Were they protesting vegans?
The grammar and punctuation needed help
And Johnny erased a whole skyscraper with her imagination
And then did an apologetic against
Inventing your own truth

Johnny put on a plastic mac
You know the ones, they are yellow and shiny

Othniel Poole

The students at uni got really upset
And then it started raining
And they were even more irate

We huddled in a replica World War 2 bunker
And pretended we were in Germany
Trying to get Hitler to repent
We saw Dietrich Bonhoeffer sneaking around
And we put him in a straightjacket
And sent him to India to see Gandhi

We then watch Rabbi K. A. Schneider on the TV
He was preaching about the idea
That God can be so in love with you
That He gets confused
It's in the Song of Solomon, in a translation
That's not the most common
But Rabbi speaks Hebrew better than Meshuggah like us

Johnny climbed Everest in a crayon drawing she'd done
She showed me and the teacher put it on the wall
I took a piece of apple, and shoved it my mouth
So it looked like my teeth were one huge piece
Of granny smith

We ate patties of beef free beef in peace
By there were no peas
I think you've heard that before if you were paying
Attention. Attention!

This is your captain speaking
Johnny is serving coffee in your campus
And she wants to guide you into the right career
Without rancour and without shame
Or humiliation
You may know her
But she might be using a pseudonym
Like Badus Mechodia
Or Beshada Jehanna
Or Nipat Ventomo
But you'll know it's her
Just by looking her
In those beautiful
Hazel
Eyes!

Praise be the LORD GOD of Israel
Whose Son is Jesus Christ of Nazareth
Who died on a cross at Calvary
For our sins, where we have missed the target
And he has spread the good word into hearts
That were open, for eternal life
Come to Him and make your home with Him
And you will find Peace, Peace, where there was none
Monks have searched, and Cardinals gone red
But the Word of Jehovah lasts
Forever. Be with Him as we worship
And you will be baptised

In water and the Spirit
And live 1000 years with Him
Upon the Earth
CLEANING IT UP
And it will be for His delight
And Johnny and I will watch over you
As you build forts
And wrestle in the playground of reality
And there will be no drugs
Either for recreation or relief of pain, not a single pill

Kelly Is A Wakeup Call

2nd January 2019

Kelly, Kelly
Hear your songs upon the MTV
You give my girlfriend strange ideas
Please write a song so she'll stay in with me
You have such a lovely voice
Your dark side helps me see
But I love my woman so
Please guide our stream and keep us a to b
I love you, Kelly Clarkson
I now too get just what I want
Heartbreak does such funny things
It makes you back to front
I'm sorry that this city boy
Has been a cure all runt
But God bless you for all you sing
To hopeful you mean everything
A O A O AO
And so we reach beach echoing
To hopeful you mean everything

I Wait For You

25/9/2002

Sitting at a picnic table
Down off Victoria Street

I wait for you

Sitting at the table
Knuckles rapping out a beat

I wait for you

Clouds grow thick above my head
Wish I was somewhere else instead
Waiting is a bore I dread
But still I wait for you

I wait for you

Time gets late, it's half past one
Frustration grows, in wasted time

I wait for you

The winds whip up, the cars go by
With still no luck, yet like a fool

I wait for you

Today I could be having fun
Are you sure you said we'd meet at one?
All this wait should be done
But no. I wait for you

I wait for you

Were you the blonde passing in a car
It would help a bit if I knew who you are
At the very least, you know, you could have rung
I have better things that could be done
Than wait for you.

Why do I get the feeling I've been stood up?
Why do I even bother

To wait for you

Some people are walking over
Maybe they would like my seat

I wait for you

I'll wait for 20, then I'll leave
I'm sad, I'm grieved, bereaved, fig leaved
Still, there's not point in being grieved

You will return

22nd December 2019; Anno Domini

Amaxzing Blue Sue Chi And Edom Jakson The Cub

AMAXZING BLUE SUE CHI AND EDOM JAKSON THE CUB

By Matthew Poole

Contents:

1: Enezhi Nation

2: Poison (With Extra Whipped Soy Sauce)

3: Crew P

4: The Sultans Of Grapes

Chapter One:
Enezhi Nation

22nd December 2019

Today, this is what happened a minute before you started reading:

Quasars and pulsars gushed and gaping war and warm maw, this was the blood of a million worlds coming together. There was no fear and there was no land, there was no Earth and there was no moisture. The gods ah... they had helped no one, for there had been none created to help.

Leftover from a billion universes before was a strange red lion called Edom Jakson. He flew thrugh the debris and ate melons and duckewedd. He was awesome and stately and righteous and noble and ture. I loved to listen to him speak, and he was a good man of high standing. If you can call a lion a man. Why, he was heir to everything, but nothing had been created yet.

There came a woman to see Edom Jakson, a spirit named Blue Sue Chi, and she was an Azurite.

"Woo you," said Edom, not know what he asayu.

"Be you too," said Sue.

"To be we so to?" said Em.

"Beck mind du sip wip," said Sue.

And this went on for about 14 munurws.

We watched as Sue and Ed wended their way through yhr potentials of a thusnad would s and then they told their gface rto establish right standing with the worlds they had left behind in order to start the strue world of ta housand woyulds. And so it began:

"Let there be bubbles!" said we.

And there was bubbles, and Sjue saw that the bubbles were good and seperated the bubbles from thr weird acrimony of a thousands publerives worlds. An d there was evening and there was dawn, a new world.

And this wotld was called AEnezki Natioon, because before there thad been no enrereegy.

Chapter 2:
Posion. (With Exyra Whipped Soy Sauce)

And Edom Jakson spoke to the Ezekinu who lie in the depths of nations unspoke n of even in legenfs, foe they are like Eedooi from the Berliy. And this is what they said towards the lion:

"We have behled you a thousand years," Edom, "And we now that you care for us with a million bbell etremeis. And it is expedient that you watch for our wors and dictate wsall that you hear into the ears of the black foundtry feepetr."

And Edom would not, in Jesus Name.

Chapter 3:
Crew P

On the waters of the sea were the watertank twins. They were named Obe and Oba. Obe was black but painted himself white and Oba was red. Obe was male, Oba was female. Obe had a hammer that he took out wonkywhoops with. The wonkywoops were pigzeuses that Shraten the Damned had planted on the oceans like a kinf of bluegeen amal scum.

Shraten lived in the tree of the sea, which was shrouded in a peculiar gog of wisdom. The gog of wisdom would lure seacars into its fog and then reareanged them in to seagsheo. The seagsheo would flock around Obe and he would lead them to pastures of kelp through the narrow door.

Oba liked to look at the leaves on the bottom of the trenches of the ocean, where all the weird woopplegoongs lied. She would read them, like a map, and then she would tell Sue Chi.

"That's marveloous, " saif Saue Ci.

"Wow, I'm so glad youthink so," said Obbs.a.

"Would you like a duck for breakfast?" asked Sue Chi.

"Why, yes?" said Oa, but what is a duck?

"WAjm jshe ih A duck is a veyu l."

Chapter 4
The Sultans Of Grapes

"Hello," said Sue Chi, "I have gone to Earth and I have gone to the pub ANNE-Tipsycocktails, and now I am cured of being a goddess. May you all not be as delusional as I was. I love you so so much. I just want to hug everybody and dance. I want to talk and talk and talk and play video games on my phone. I want to praise Jesus Christ and rat on a melon. WEhop de boot. OOF. Flurph! Pardon my Dutch. And we'll go to the Netherlands and eat a wienyouf."

And then Oba said "you are the most sensible person I have ever heard. You are equal to Winston Churchill, Charlemagne, Smith Wigglesworth and Buddha."

Better to have loved and won, than to sit on the street.

Love your friend Matthew Poole.

See you next chapter! :)

Passion Of Luther Maundy

25th December 2019
10:27PM

If you can look into my heart, what will you see? Layers of drugs, layers of dreams, layers of passion and false fatherhoods, stakes and claims and broken women breaking my trust. If you can look that way, you see the past, but that's the wrong way.

To the future, Luther Maundy

The fanatics are outside in Eden

Hipsters with broken hearts

Crumbling their clozapine over the grave of Mary McKillop

Taking their dirty underwear to the cliffs of Flinders and throwing them over like lemmings

Reading theology books backwards and then playing them in a mashup of Laura Jean.

Breaking bread with a cyborg who is trying to figure out where your bread is on their GPS.

Dancing with Siri while hacking into her braces so she can have better blueteeth.

To see Christ bearing his visceral heart before the milk as the meat comes tumbling in.

Seeing the sushi of the Lord come down and make actions before the smiley faces of whom.

Blood on the plz maut woop demat black spack reason democrat.

The great breakdown is in reverse.

The engineers work on this puzzle together.

Make an example of him!

But at least I seek the true thing.

Frustration, people looking for humility.

People looking for revenge for someone who is just a concept to them.

A myriad of patchwork mirrors of whom they saw a parody of themself.

But I am skin and not a silver mirrorball.

But still you can dance with me to Darude in demure politness and hardcore NRG.

And you can be clean.

I cleaned my words.

And now you have it.

But at least I said it.

I said my peace.

Boxing day.

Will I find friends who don't want to put me in their concept.

Who don't want me to fight their wars?

I'm going to heaven.

Does anyone think.

Dillinger thinks hard.

And Woodward thinks with tempremament.

Rietveld thinks with the history of philosophers.

Bruton thinks with a lens of optomitrist's soap boxes.

Love is tender.

That's all.

Passport Soon, Cuddles For Now

7th October 2019

    It is good to praise the Lord

    And worship til you're out of breath

    And then awake in eagerness

    To face another action day

When you give your all to God, what else is there? It's a new morning, and you just want to be held. You wander the local streets, and wonder who really knows you. You want to bring the Kingdom, but what are you bringing them to? They have houses, cars, education, everything they need in life. But they don't have you, do they? What are they going to do with you? Are they going to send the pharmaceutical nurse out to coddle you after you have prophesied? Are they going to check your bags and find Bibles and birth certificates when you just went in there to pick a Kanzi apple? Are they going to talk to you as they maintain the machines? Are they going to stare as you eat you Lindt Mint Creation chocolate, unsure if this is a return to Genesis?

The roads are long. Every tree is blessed, every branch worthy of a story from JEHOVAH. Sometimes it appears like a digital simulation. Where is everybody?

There are toys in the kid's shop window. That's not my flamingo. My flamingo doesn't have a shiny beak. That's not my monkey. That's not my panda. I thought about buying That's Not My Panda, but I wasn't sure if the soft toy was my panda. And I hadn't shaven so I thought I'd better look respectable before entering the nursery. I'm a lumberjack and I'm okay.

And after a night of worship and peace with God, you just want cuddles. Where are my entourage? I can understand how a man like

Solomon needed so many around him, after Wisdom, who can compare?

My body aches and I don't know whether it is a sin to ache. I have my picture taken but I look nothing like it, the cafe says that blind dating's like that.

So much writing, so much gospel, so much learning, where are the wombs of mind and soul and heart to take this implantation?

I wander into a park and sit on a bench in my Bermuda t-shirt. I wonder if people think I'm lost. After such connection with God, why do I feel like I do the next day?

Holy Spirit cuddled me this morning. I'm very soft and sweet, really. I got a rejection letter from a really conveniently placed job. They said there was no room for me. But I am welcome to drink their coffee and have a chat.

Family is the most beautiful thing in the world. What is institutionalised mess? People want identity, they want to be unique. ELEGANT HAGEN wrote a reminder about Ephesians on my phone. Despite what the accusing soapboxers say, I have never worshipped Diana.

I want to go to the Moon. I want to go there and raise a family and we can have wind farms and solar panels and a great compost heap and lots of fingerpaint. And cows. The cows of the moon. We can meet those lunar people that the 18th century Bishop wrote about who love to worship when an Earthling mentions the name of Jesus.

I have so many good books. Franz Kafka stands out. Wowsers, he's funny. It's like reading my mail. I saw a book about a surprise rival in the laundromat, and I saw your full name on a book next to it.

Saw a family friend on the bus. They have given me a wonderful book of poems, lots of female poets. She asked if I had a favourite, and I wanted to say someone I hadn't known before this book, but I hadn't grown that familiar with them. It's like being on Walhalla's high cricket pitch without a ball.

Deep Wisdom. Holiness and purity. Spreading the Kingdom. Do come into my house when I have laid it out. Do come in, deaf and blind, down's and asperger's, poor and mad and wanting to go on guided UFO tours, ripping up playing cards and turning CD cases inside out and playing cowboys and indians with them, as if there were cowboys all over the Hindu continent. Yee Hah!

Tender community. Unpresentable parts of society. Into the tent you go.

Passport soon, and I'll be visiting the world.

Cuckolopolis And The Orkney Androids

29th January 2020
8:38PM

When I was a child, I listened hard to the sound of snails at mu mailbox. I loved the sound of thunder in the morning. I listened with bated breath for the smell of putrid perfume that I didn't appreciate til I was older. All seven senses I hear in sound. So thats septero.

I don't know why the mutton kids go on about junk on the bus. They are servants of Lord Razor, who is married to Molly Middenbark. Raze the Lord, I say. Set him on Fire.

Molly Middenbark is beautiful, she carried a crescent of lightbulbs around her neck, and she's the skin of a German wilderness.

But Lord Razor is constantly driving into us kids. Like he tries to plough us down with his car.

I list my list that I am going to tell my sweetheart, Gruesome Figwitch.

My name is Handsoe Mangel.

I am artistic, and I sturggle to speil well and sometimes I steam like a boat full of rowing.

"Who da king?" said the alpha of the mutton kids, whose name was Bruford Manpure.

"We are very lucky not to have to worry about politics," I said, "we just have to rely on childhood romance. What's wrong with you, Bru?" I laughed. "I must calm down, but she's waiting for my bus to stop."

We stopped at a dusty station, a lazy caterpillar like corrugated iron in olive bottle green and just as stuffed. I was dropped off, and Gruesome Figwitch, the love of my life, is there with Molly Middenbark.

"Why, Handsoe," said Molly, "Gu finds you very attractive."

"Kind of you to see that," I said, "but I must be alone with my lady, you are grown up and you don't understand our ways without getting very plastered on white russians and playing pop music from the age of the meltdown of the cold war."

"Well, we can't all be on our high horse," said Molly, "what brings you to Gruesome tonight?"

"He loves me," said my little Figgy pudding.

"Does he?" remarked Molly, and put on some lipstick, "Why does he love you? What does he know about company?"

"He knows about factories!" said Figgy. "His Dad works at the icehouse where they freeze the meat."

"Meat is for vegetables who haven't evolved," said Molly.

"Why do veggies eat meat?" asked Figgy.

"Stop contradicting," said Molly, "can't you see I'm trying to pull you apart."

"I love my Figgy," I said, "you leave her alone of course or I'll write you a nasty letter."

"And what's your nasty letter going to say, Han?" asked Molly, with a sneer in her voice like a pack of wasps drinking bitter polly waffle water.

There was a gum tree that was easy to carve with my long fingernails, so I wrote two letters to this Corinthian Philistine.

"H. Y."

Figgy fainted, and Molly drew a knife on me.

"Mangling meddler," she roared, "if you knew what you were doing I'd have your throat and send you to the Orkney Islands!"

"Well, I'm getting sick of Cuckolopolis," I said, "you just think everything's about siloing yourself away and waiting for enough wheat for a harvest fist."

"Future you wouldn't say that," said Molly, "future you would follow my feet and run to Lord Razor."

"Lord Razor isn't Jesus," I said.

"What?"

"Razor isn't Jesus," I said, "and he's not a Rabbi, or Talmudic, or even a skinny cow with a scraf."

"Whatch your moth," said Molly, "I ooto boop you my groppely bubpopwemp!"

"That's the spirit," I said, "Holly Molly, it's time to celebrate, you've been born again."

And Molly fainted and Figgy bore herself aloft, and stood on her feet as if drawn up like a released catapault.

"I love you, Handsome," said Fey Jean, which is now what Gruesome Figwitch was entitled by Jesus.

"I love you, wise girl," I said, "now walk with me into the safety of the ranbow of time, an we will bolt like mend-all-you-ill."

And she kissed me on the cheek, then faster on the forehead, ran her fingers thick through my hair, pushed my back and rashed me into the horizon until you and me were you and your sweetheart. God bless you, children.

9:04PM

Ecce Leise Ace Says

**29th January 2020
12:50AM**

Eve is so black, but it's because of my peppercorns;
I mushed them up and put them across her eyelids;
That is true eyeshadow;
I'd rather it was blue;
But it's well to do;
Today I lived a thousands years;
Walking down the banks of the Murray;
And when I give my books to study;
Then new ideas are growing, burning;
Stirring with their fists and dreaming;
Of the live they'll live;
When they are forgiven;
And their song is parted from the caterpillar;
Born again;
I told her that I love her;
I told her where to look to hear those words;
But she's reading shapes;
She doesn't see the lobes of lips;
She doesn't see my political Saint Francis
Conservative of Whips;
Merge me with my dreams;
I know she spills parallel beans;
I didn't know she had supplies;

And I realise that's my wry wise;
Adonai tells me to greet;
And Abba instructs on the street;
People growing fat on mock;
Mean to go sup some mead;
Be my entry point, o son
Get the glory work all done
And you will run and run and run
Your gun will speak about the kine
And your thin horses will dibine
And your thin daises with the qune.

Leonard Tulip And The Dimples

29th December 2019

By Othniel Poole the Baptist

El Shaddai was teaching his people;
He listed their sins and they felt bad;
And then he tapped them on the shoulder;
And after that... what fun they had!
Adonai was making gravy
For the chickens and the goose
And Haman was acting badly
Wanting to tie shoes with noose
And there I was, alone, afraid
And looked at all the beds unmaid
To my king I offered praise
But demons taught me to offer up
Reparation mayonnaise
And who would hurt a starving child
And teach them to forever crave?
Who would list books as ignorance
For the sake of saving Dave?
Why it was Leonard Tulip
Leonard Tulip was his name
I will say it again
Get it in your neurons and your chemical transmitters and let us not be bitter;
Thank you

The Letters of Tabula

His name was Leonard Tulip

Leonard Tulip was his name

He was a man of mighty fame

And yet obscured by bust flames

Remember for God's sake

That Leonard Tulip was his name

And he was a wonderful sort

He took the tennis balls to court

And then he hit them with his bat

And everyone applauded him

And he wanted to see the world

And it would be divided

Because of him

Because of his revelation

How he bared his heart to nations

Leonard Tulip was his name

And not Othniel Poole the Baptist;

Sometimes there is animation on the ice

Sometimes there's a merry daisy chain

Sometimes there's an ex Stacey

But Leonard Tulip prays you crazy!

He loved to listen to music

But after he had found a man

Who on Damascus blinded him

He decided to only sing

Of a name above all the names

Even though The Lord has many monikers

You need to Moniker, when you're an Augustine

When you're drunk and still drinking

Othniel Poole

You need a nurse, you need a guide
You need a brownie, open wide!
Leonard Tulip had wild hair;
Look at that radical air?
And when you're at the tree of life
Pick a pair
And feel medium rare
Well done
For God so loved the world
That he gave a man who didn't have a home
That he gave a man who liked to listen to the ladies
And when the blowhard men came on
He told them about their dirt inside their cups
And how they were oft filled with bones
And then he trashed their home
And Leonard Tulip loved to talk
Of being high on A-on-i
And being intimate with Christ
While protesting gays at night
And he was into rock and roll
And he had a band
Do you remember the name of this here man?
It was not Othniel Poole
It was not any baptist, fool
It was a man who questioned Fudd
Because he wanted rabbits to abound
Remember this: what was his name?
Leonard Tulip: zenith of alleged
Let's forgive him, set him straight

Before the demons vacillate
Leonard Tulip headlining
The Arrow Knowledge Concerto
And this is what you need to know
Leonard Tulip's act upon Marquee:
LEONARD TULIP AND THE DIMPLES
Arise to God and pop your zits
And we will blow cathedrals into pieces
And then when there is no peace
We'll sign the seven season lease
In Nuremberg they yelled and wept
And told that we must all be same
That we must be perfect
As the Lord is
And then they killed our kids
The Dimples were a big brass band
And sometimes hard to understand
They needed to go learn to read
But a little air is what they need
So they gave up their cigarettes
And had some chocolate with orbs
Hollows like the cave
Of Joseph Arim's hotel grave
Let us pray for Tulip now
Let his wife hunger for text
Until they learn to read some more
And talk in live streams less!
God bless Leonard Tulip
Lord bless him keep him, every hair

Let his children prosper

Now and forever

God bless Leonard Tulip's wife

Just for God's sake put away the knife

For Laughter is no longer up for slaughter

Be a giggle daughter!

Amen

I love people of the world

I love listening to tales

I love all the languages

Even when their beliefs

Are violent and off the rails

I love tongues and I love Latin

Remember language

And prophecy

And monikers

Are pattern; Selah;

AO at the children of HOME

FOOTNOTE:

Reading is vital. Reading is the gift God gave man. Reading is what makes the Ten Commandments great. You see yourself in the shapes and figures of the letters, and you realise: "hey, I'm not so great after all." Whatever you write that judges judges you. Whatever you say has meanings in languages you do not know. God reveals through his Spirit, but he is also a master analyst.

Let water wash us clean. Because to sensitive skin, fire disfigures and makes the handsome like a horror. I was clean; but I still had a cup that needed cleaning. So I took paper and I wrote my dirt, and then I put it where the water flowed.

Let this be a bomb. Push the button and move on.

29th December 2019
ANNO DOMINI
12:08PM

(Part Variable of Infinity)

24th February 2020
5:53PM

So, frere, pain in the heart; this is what it means to be a white fool. This is what it means to be the tricky dirk; this is what it means to be a knife without covenant; this is what it means to be a father-in-law that wants a likely story so he can cover his tracks with a remix of light and wonder and a phat beat for the drums of the east; drums that count out three million gods and requite a split twin who goes to the top and asks them to talk down and generate their specials so much to the children.

This is Laban's tale:

I wandered sheepishly through dreams and actions and motions and phortresses and actions and waspings and lotions and backwards whoops and motion gumption established holy write by far and honest dealings of soft white motion; and this be the riddle of holy established kine and beautiful pseudo-dross that is really the crumbs from the children's table reassembled by dogs not into a dog god of their own image, nor of a fox at the table of apocalypse, but of a muffin of an African design; pumperkicker and borderfull.

So Laban: what do you have for use?

This is my friend; this is my friend. This is my friend the wonder-dog; the glory of a million years. Righteous, peace and goy and the Ewelly Guest.

Slow down;

What did you learn, Patrick?

Patrick learnt that days go by and breathing is what you need to live and move and have your being. Oklahoma is divise (diverse) and love is a hopeful thing. How we long for the end of days, but have we been knighted thoroughly enough to take on the full moon and her savage smiles?

Rush nicht; rush nicht; for you do not know what the next minute will bring forth; bring fifth; bring sea and spirit, but together; both as one. Bring the dove upon the Jordan and let Jesus Christ, the Lord of All, say just who he is to the people who have come, cut to the heart, with their two tunics shining in the sun and let them give him a towel and let them see the Lamb with holiness and majesty and established writ of glory, and let them whisper their questions they are too afraid to ask the ones with foreheads like pyrite dressed as flint.

I have deigned myself a place in the fields of glory; what is this? And for what was this child meant for; this child born fraternally with two twin girls, a red and hairy man who lives in the twin states and whose children win the hearts of both Israelis and Palestinians until all are red and hairy?

Eh, what?

And we live and move and have our being in him. That's what a stadium concert means

Love, live, and eat your bread with thankfulness, and let us find a real substitute for milk. We cannot sow questions forever, we cannot; so let's rise and watch and find something where we can approach one another over crimson coffee and dreadlocked pretzels to celebrate the mighty generals; I am were and so I remember. Someone has to, lest we repeat that really dreary episode of the great story, the one of whaling and kings of Edom and of conversations outside the kindegarten about alcohol, and bold brash manly debaters in the face of romantics, and of revolutions in cyan towns; and musicals in animations; and topical episodes that make no sense in 2 months time; and sola minutae' amen

Doctel Opel

25th December 2019
8:24PM

Gaza, 1929.

I reach for a bottle of thin blue liquor and I take a swig. "It's no good, it's no good," he says, but keeps bragging about his purchase. Johnny Routledge is coming to investigate the murder by the sea, and I'm not entirely sure what he's going to find.

Johnny is a class A psycho. Tic or path, I am not entirely certain. A bit of a tictac paddy whack give the dog a sorbet with a dollop of passionfruit. That's the way love goes. Allegedly, not until proven in a court of law.

I brush my hair sideways, so that the long, lanky bits that are blonde reach square with the short cut hair of the sides of my head. I take a quipu and tie it on the edge of a bollard, leaving three aluminium tags in the winter sunlight.

Johnny is gathering blackberries from a copy of the Torah that has rotten and has become soil partly, but the thing is the soil keeps going and going and going. Sophie Charlotte Dexter is asking us for a million shekels, but I'm not entirely sure she knows what a shekel is. Abstract passions can be deciduous.

So are we going to get to this murder? I am observing a million things and if I saw the sign of obsidian crimson I think I'd be so sick that I'd grow about 14 extra dimensions in the tachyon neurosystem plantward wad gourmand.

He is in heaven, and you are on Earth, so let your words be few.

I walk through Gaza, and I truly consider walking to Egypt. Jesus spent time in Egypt, so I'm not after to eat of the coffins of Coptics. Jesus left, he outgrew the place quicker than Cushy Moses.

Sophie Charlotte Dexter is reading a map pinned to a wall. It is full of convict portraits with great grins on their faces with the phrase:

WE HATE PAIN BUT WE WORK HARD UNTIL WE FEEL PAIN

WE MAKE PERFECT SENSE

And she went right up to the map and she licked it with a rough and wide tongue, like it was the stamp of the correspondence of Atlas.

"Do you have to do that here in Gaza, Soph?" I moaned, throwing a screwed up copy of the paper at her. The headline of that one had read "Recession means a half hour break to play in the sandpit."

Johnny started putting up fences in Gaza. He has a tape measure and he is weeding out weeds and throwing them into the ocean between the pinky on his right hand and his ring finger. There is no ring so he takes a lump of clay and stains the top of where the ring should be with it. Then he wipes the rest of the clay in Sophie's face.

"That's remarkable, like something out of Moby Grape," she said, and proceded to extend the borders of Gaza to Virginia, Maryland and Rhode Island in her imagination which gave her diplomatic immunity in some Sepher dimension or another.

There was a human navel the size of a cauldron in the centre of Gaza, and a lot of the Gazans were looking into it and throwing down the carcasses of turkeys, canaries, and french wrens.

This is very curious...

Johnny and Sophie were now holding hands and descending into the navel. They appeared in the heavens with two wands of cedar sawn oak and ate the wedding cake of a thousand hypothesis.

Blessed are the merciful for they shall obtain mercy.

The man in a van said to the Beatles that Gaza this year was frightfully signficant. I believe it when the Proverbs man says that those that lie in wait for blood are not your friends.

At least, the corpswe.

It was the corpse of a female, red hair, freckles on her shoyllders, going blue like the colour of a bruise as if a glase on a Chinese dish. She was facedown in the Gazan dirt.

We shall have to give an account for every deed done in the body, whether good or bad. That's a number, a calculation, a negotiation.

Abstractions were calculating again, and I felt the wasping wisps of a million nether nations come forth, and the Monk with his eyes established in Leeds took his magnifying glass and handed it to me with a flick of the wrist, which turned on a switch which shone the light onto the corpse of the female with the auburn and blue and musk of Sheol.

She woke up and rose, covering her raw areas with crossed arms.

She was dangerous like that.

"And so your case is over," she said.

"Blue remarks," I mused.

Johnny put a gun to my head.

"You having enough of Mergeurtroi?" he said.

"Leave him along Nok." said Sophie Charlotte.

And then I realised it was actually 1948.

I had been, and I'd been canned, and this was all on film. So special in the valley of the dhaow of death, and I feel no fieval.

Black wandering mercy righteous wind duck passion seizure.

And that was the code that led me into the heart of Jerusalem, where I bathed of this muck for another day, and I got to have a day with my wife, kids, orphans, relatives and Jesus Christ.

And he sung to me:

So well you are

And known to me

The Letters of Tabula

Dirt sticks for a day
But water lasts longer
And what is water
But ant

Tenylee Bruce and Bruce Tenyeel

13th February 2020
10:10PM

Police were resting with their dreams

On the beach and lazing idly

And there Tenylee Bruce decided

That he'd meet his frame boyd

And that boyd was Bruce Tenyeel

And they looked at the plam, that is to say the plan

And they opened up a great wingspan

And there upon their silver bird

They ate up every white rapt curd

And then when they returned to Earth

They were filled with pale blue mer

And when the fill came in a line

They spoke the worse and made some more

And then they healed themselves

And became much better

Gentle Tenylee

Became

Twentyman Spark

Pamela The Wise

23rd January 2020
2:30PM

Love you, Pamela the Wise
With the knight of a thousand jelly mersons
Love you so, look in your waiting
Look at what you're instigating
Love you day and love you night
Love you in peace and the fight
Pamela let's do this right
Pamela let us be like French
And be so very nice
And costs will come and that's okay
I will pay them all the way
And if people call me too grin
Then I in joke will let them in
And I say to you, my swop
Let me be in chicken shop
Let me read you my shirt top
And let me Glassnost Bop
And let me go to spaghetti
And it is getting so ready
But it is so ridiculous
How do people eat this stuff?
And let me go to baker's avenue
How the bread grows from the vine

Othniel Poole

I do not have a clue
But I know that when I sit with you
And you hold me linked in arm
Just over the bed
Like a cliff
And like a parapet
I know that I am well and wise
Because I trust you with my kiss
And because, of course, of this
Then I can give you all
My grouped up burstwit grocery list
And Pamela, you funny one
Let me give you all the planets
In... what can I day?
I mean... what can I say?
You want me to implain it?
And love me so, and dear, love you
And I want to be supplying in my buying and my crying
But for you alone do I be coin
And to you my inheritance
I do as carpenter would do
And I would cease
And then you will see me
And my Father is always with me
So let's go together
Let's get away
And choose any path
For genetically, the people's of the world
Are more than just a graph

And I am more than random integers
Let me stomach all that you infer
And I will grow, but not fat sou
Let me be the one to street about
Half thinking but more spirit fed
And when the pilot is cast in
Then he will need
After he composes
To find a merry seat
And look out at all the gadgets
And say So beside the co-pile
O, the days that we shall sail
Oh the days of mop and pail
Oh the days of hill and veil
And oh the pays and oh the riesling
Pamela, I am never teasing
2:42PM

Hidden Frustration

**15th January 2020
8:50AM**

I know that it hurts

And you wonder about them

I know that you grieve

When they walk away

But they speak from their anger

And hidden frustration

They don't want to sell out their Lord

The guns in the parlour

Are soft and alluring

Machetes at weddings

Are gleaming and new

And I don't desire

To carve up the bacon

When there are trees full of life

And we're trying so hard

The people of Zion

The people who take

All the sadness away

And we want to go with you

But we are alarmed

We thought we all

Were okay

And we have decided

That we will risk seven
And we have decided
To fire the stones
And we have decided
To send our best man
Into the light
To eat pie
And life is a duckweek
And life is a knife
And life is a pleasure
When toys are your life
And life is a happen'
All shiny and new
But people come on
With their software

Captain Lion

30th October 2019

Good friend
Good friend who sat next to me
Good friend who got used to me
When I went on and on and on
Who joked with me using other people's songs
Who let me play songs through the phone
Who let me tell repetitive jokes
Who let me shake my albums and play with the images
Of pop icons
Who drove with me
Who yearned for travel
Who was interesting in who I had a crush on
Who was my crush; Selah

I don't believe in Liberals
I don't believe in Surgery
I don't believe in Pharmacy
I just believe in Captain Lion
Captain Lion and me
My church and my family
And that's my reality

Eternity has begun
What can I say?

Reykjavic Raga On Inferno Of Destinicore

21st October 2019

No instruction in the day of the forage. No instruction in the day of the forage.

Woe to everyone who picks on their porridge. No instruction in the day of the forage.

Exploitation, collectors, big destruction, bad actors, evil rationing, starving kids

Did you do as Lord Messiah did!

Get on your knees, into the mud

Create a man from all the cud

No instruction in the day of the forage. No instruction in the day of the forage.

Take away all you've given as sorrows. Take away all you've given as arrows.

Develop your mind and leave all promise behind, observe yourself and the stars will all shine

Untied it is time not to keep it together; protest the children and express their gaols;

Send them into space; see the Face of Elohim; the God of Israel with a fist full of cuppa gin;

No instruction in the day of the forage; it all hinges on the One you adorage.

And the wicked will burn with the tungsten black wrath; and Yeshua will adopt the aftermath!

No instruction in the day of the forage; selah

Feunib Smith says what she sees

Feunib Smith knows enemies

Feunib Smith makes peace with all

Feunib Smith will for eternity myself will call and we'll be as them. Amen; selah++aoe

Marrying An Anthrobram

October 18 2018

Superstar bigger than Lady Gaga and a man that was burn asway and stayed;

See inside his slick cosmos, know about his quintuplets, and weep for yourself in the mansions of

Heaven's Soul. Going to jail for a vision because he wants to see where Ned Kelly had a joke;

Adar is making prophecies and she's a keeper of time; only trouble is she's frightening the world;

Superstar as glorious as someone who interprets such a word as glorious though it's used in praise;

He has an encounter with Light and he inspires the chocolate marketing campaign;

Selah

Russian cuddles at midnight and someone eats a stick of broccoli with almond butter and that is diet;

What's this got to do with someone as mysterious as An Anthrobram? Do you hear her Name?

Anthrobram is lovely and she is quite green and experienced in piercing men and making them sue;

She's a lawyer of sorts, she's the queen of tarts; yes she knows Mordialloc Warts;

When you go to the pennies that you saved and you realised that they always have a flute to play;

When the Superstar declares his name is now Peter Anthrobram, he shaves his collar bone and A;

He has passed the test, now he must not be careless but raise ELOHIM so high that he separates

Firmament from the red grapes, bramble in the pocket and he don't know how to stop it like a white

Russian. Drinking so deeply that you read with your eyebrows like a Dr Seuss prophecy. What's

That to do with me? I try so pooling resources to understand the Superstar, he's red faced and

Standing on His own shoulders like a therapist with methadone eating; the panettone;

Touching my Complete Works of William Wordsworth/Library Eponymous/Sauce Code Geronimous

As you reach for the doctor's grey's anatomy there is a caddice working surely to the friend;

Mongrels become princesses in the end.

And the smooth shape of such a star, free of thorns and blooming so wonderfully, travelling the Ea;

Games of action and delight and there's no more choking but there's plenty of jest! I attest that I

Passed and the Woman of My Dreams…

HIDEOUS TORMENTS

October 18 2019

Awareness of time is key
We do as we have done
But seers say be a lake
And twins, I am not sure
But do they fight?

My Punishment Is More Than I

October 16 2019

My punishment is more than I
My arms outstretched, that's one thing done
My punishment is more than I
When One finds me, then I die
My punishment is more than I

Herb and grass they flee from me
A merry chain of daisies, see?
Herb and grass they flee from me
I know hope's opportunity
Herb and grass they flee from me

Elohim he left a Mark
I read it every day and dark
Elohim he left a Mark
And matrimony in the park
Elohim he left a Mark

Accusing me called Nodding Dude
And the car's contents is my food
Accusing me called Nodding Dude
And the rod and staff renewed
Accusing me called Nodding Dude

I build a city for the sun
And light will shine on every Hon
I build a city for the sun
It can't be hid or rid of fun
I build a city for the sun

I walk the Earth a wanted man
It feels so good to know I can
I walk the Earth a wanted man
Who will reward you for the globe's capture
And here we are, an unexpected rapture

I leave a legacy in Genes
Average is what it means
I leave a legacy in Genes
When I wander from the lines
I leave a legacy in Genes

I'm so glad, My Father
You didn't stop me like Adam
And like Abraham, unlike I mean
You didn't cut me off before my time
You didn't stop me like Adam + Of course them will = I CAN BEAR
Let's raise some wheat and burn the tare!
We have reached the end of age
Let's Herald the Son
Good News, Good News
Cain has found a wife!
Cain has uncovered a life!

Where Abel was dissed

This One is kissed!

Praise is Californian Riot!

Draft this wordy drink and try it! HalleluYah and Sweetness

Teal and cyan

And this is word

Question me

Rosy Tot:

By:

Matthew Othniel Poole

Written:

26th - 27th March 2020 ace ad

Fun Facts:

Originally this had the working title of *Total Delirium* and I thought of *Totes Delirium* too - after listening to the song *Quartet* by ABWH a couple of times; where they mention the Yes song "Gates of Delirium" and the whole pathogen zeitgeist in March 2020 going on. However, it's much nicer, and since it's a story about very small children in need of love and protection from danger to be called "Rosy Tot", it's really lovely, and I've been feeling really mellow and loved and safe writing it.

Contents:

1: Fragile, She's Dizzy

2: Precious Wind, Seeds, Fruit, Sister

3: Beset By Friends Met From Food

4: Morning Dins (Anna And Redorthy)

5: Weapons of Nightmares

6: Waiting For... And Something Unexpected

7: Darcee And Her Nap

1: Fragile, She's Dizzy

Written: 26th March 2020 (5:33PM)

In her straw hat; Little Tabula Rosa looked very pleased with herself with all her journals.

"Look what I've done, Daddy," she said, and pointed to all her notebooks; unlined as yet and all filled with writings.

There was **StoryCity**; **Gogoboy**; and **Beview Picture Stories**.

Her father; growing a beard and scratching his lengthening hair; scoured over the documents.

"And you wrote these?" he asked.

He scanned the name of the front of the journals.

"**Otto S. Prayservoir**?" he giggled, "Oh, Tabs, you are funny."

Toto was her first name; but it had nothing to do with being little or beastly; and much more about being absolutely everything to her parents; and being a little one who stands up in the face of danger and sings her heart out.

It was prophetic because she hadn't worked up to a lot of danger yet; as she was very small.

"Where did you get these ideas from?" asked her father.

"I get them from what's funny," said Toto, nudging her father as hard as she could with her elbow; and since she was so small it was barely a pudgy tickle in his shin.

"A riot of humour," said her father, "are you telling the truth when you write though?"

"It's a story," whined Tabula, "it's from my dreams."

"But you want your dreams to be true," said her father, "so they'd better be the truth."

"How can they be the truth beforehand?" asked Tabula.

"Out of love, there is truth," said Dad.

"And how do I know if I'm loving and not being selfish like when I hog the dishes at dinner with Darcee?"

Darcee was Toto's sisteress; she was a very good cook at even such an early age; though sometimes Toto took the dishes because she wanted to help so much. She was so full of energy and gave everything she had. Some darling onlookers said she was giving way too much too early.

"A tot martyr is the sloop of tragedies," said one of the parents of the village green where they lived. It was called Boone Readimus, the town.

"What's a sloop?" asked Tot.

"It's where you want to go home," said her Dad.

"Really?" said Toto, "That sounds wonderful. I want to go home all the time."

"Be careful what you wish for," said her father.

"Dad?"

"Yeah, Tots?"

"What's the difference between a wish and a prayer?"

"More negotiation in a prayer," said her Father, "genies and the like don't generally want to be your friend after a wish, they'd much rather get back to their oil and their light and their confines."

"So a non-genie asks to answer a prayer?" said Tot, and she was thinking very hard, even harder than when she was writing.

"Yes,"

"And what non-genie do I ask to say my prayer?"

"I don't know, Tabula; some words are a bit neglected. Some people reckon that if you don't believe a word has a meaning, then you shouldn't use it."

"But I like to talk about dragons and raisin-people and dog-wobble-whoompie-beans," said Tots.

"Yes, you do, don't you?" smiled her father, giving her a one armed cuddle and looking out over their backyard with scooters made of plastic and toy telephones and rubber vinyl long players that worked in fantasy but not in the record collectors practicums.

"I like to talk about things I've never seen," Tabula sighed.

"In your mind's eye," said her Dad, "in there, because you want to see them. And people are made with some sense that their dreams come true."

"How do you know that, Dad?"

"Because I met your mother," said her Dad, "and I got a job as a Bushranger of this amazing land, and I had no idea how it happened, and... and... and... this nice house and your sister and mates at the cafe."

"And you dreamt all this when you were a boy?"

"I dreamt in metaphor," said her father, "and I often wrote things too."

"That's lovely," said Tots, resting in her father's side, "that's so lovely it makes me want to have cordial and biscuits and share some damper with my sister."

"Well, when your mother comes out I'll point her out to you," said Dad. "Keep writing, Tabula; keep writing until you are filled with dreams, and then we'll see if you can hope to find someone to answer your darling prayers."

"What's hope?" said Tots.

"Hope?"

"Yeah," said Tabula, "what is it?"

"It's something you don't have; but have set a path in your mind," said her father, "like a path in the world of water and air and thought and imagination and ghosts; and if you hold that path steady, you can walk in almost another dimension toward that thing you want. It's better than a goal, to have hope, at least in my opinion, and I'd like to think it was educated more by experience than by poetry; yes, it is a wonderful thing to have hope."

"Do you have to try really hard to have hope?" asked Tabs, "Do you have to screw up your forehead really tight and tremble and try to make it come boffin' out into real?"

"That's more like the end result of bravery, love," said Dad, "and that will come when you have a very big fear to conquer and at the penultimate point of hope."

"Well, that's good," said Tots, "because I'm just a beginner,"

"We all are," said her father, "as long as we have someone to love."

"Are you saying experts have no one to love?"

"Metaphysical for a tot, aren't you?" laughed her Dad.

"Yes," decided his daughter, almost bossily to someone she hoped to impress who she hadn't met, "yes, I want to meet more real persons."

6:10PM

2: Precious Wind, Seeds, Fruit, Sister

Written: 26th March 2020 (begun 6:30PM)

Darcee was taking Tots some cupcakes; two of them, one vanilla with a glace cherry and one a very pale pink with a real cherry.

"It'd be good if we had a third to share them with," said Tots, "a kid."

"Like to show you something, Tabby," said Darcee.

"Oh really," said Tabula, "what is it?"

"It's a tree that grew up overnight in our backyard?"

"Oh really," said Tabs, "how so?"

"It came from a seed on the wind," said Darcee, "it's a wind seed, like some seeds go by blowing, some by twirling, some even by fire; but for those ones you must be well far away when the seeds are spread our you will be too hurt for a toddler."

Darcee was one year older than Tabula, but they looked like twins. It makes all the difference.

"So what did they wind seed look like?" asked Tabula.

"Well, I imagine it looked like a bell with hollows like a lamp window on four sides, with a seal like wax over the top and bottom, with a stub where the flower was at the base, all burnt out," said Darcee.

"But you didn't see that," said Tot, "you just imagined it would look like that."

"It was an educated guess," said Darcee.

"What's the difference between that and a hypothesis?" said Tots.

"What's a hypothesis?"

"Ah," said Tots, smacking herself of the forehead with only the greasiness a kinderling can, "THAT's the difference!"

The Letters of Tabula

"Here's the tree," said Darcee, and before them it was.

"Wow,"

The tree was full of long snaking limbs, thin and grey, rising up and pale and smooth, bark that was bark without handhold or way to loose a page of it.

There was a base in the bottom, just above the trunk that was almost a stump if it wasn't for the 11 limbs that gyrated out from that central nobbly point; it was perfect for a treehouse; but Darcee and Tot were the sort of girls who were more into other things; it was just their family's style not to be into treehouses.

And there, low on the limb, was a single fruit.

Or was it two?

It kind of looked like one fruit, or one fruit that had tried to split in two but it had gotten stuck halfway through process. There were ruddy mandarine like freckles all over it which made it less but not altogether un-appetitsing. It was pink and green and had little scales where each one looked like a simple icon of lion under a little kiosk.

Tot loved kiosks, she just loved the word. It was like a Wendy House, but sometimes they had information, she often saw them in the wilderness when her dad took her on Daddy daughter bushranger at work days.

"Can we try to eat it?" asked Darcee, picking the fruit off the tree, "I'm going to boil it up and see if I can make jam."

"Be a bit quincy for me," said Tot, "and I don't think I'm that hungry without Mum and Dad with us to eat together. It's a very big fruit, see how it's almost two fruit?"

Darcee used her strong fingers to prize apart the fruit, and it was two fruit, each with an entirely covering skin. Close together, as one, but they had been two.

"What have you done, Darc'?" gasped her sister.

Darcee handed Tots her share of the whole self-whole half.

"Don't eat it Darcee," said Toto, "don't eat it, you don't know what it is."

Darcee took a bite; and Tots rammed hers into her large denim overall pocket. The suspenders with their copper clasps at the shoulders kept them in place.

6:48PM

3: Beset By Friends Met From Food

26th March 2020 ace (begun 7:00PM)

The next day Tots was with her pencils and pens and journals and papers. She had a very low red, plastic desk with very deep grooves for her pencils.

"I wish I had a pencil case," she said, "foolish cigarettes, are pencils. Need pen! Need pen!"

The fruit Darcee had picked her was sitting on her desk

And then Darcee entered.

"Have you met our new friend?" she asked.

"Who is it?" exclaimed Tots, eyes wide.

"Why, it's Otto S. Prayservoir," said Darcee, pointing next to her in the space.

"I don't see anyone," said Tabs.

"He's right here," said Darcee, "and he's so nice to me."

"But that's my name," said Toto, "that's my pen name."

"Otto says that Otto is a boy's name," said Darcee, "and that Otto is short for something and he was the one who really wrote all your stories. He's so dreamy."

"In your dreams," said Tots, rolling her eyes, "or maybe his, augh! But he's... um... she's *me*!"

"Definitely a boy," said Darcee, "he's going to marry me when I grow up. Or maybe I can grow up in his dreams and go to StoryCity and be grownups for a million years and have a quintillion children, because I'll be Queen and that's a Tilling, that's what Otto says; he calls it a Dad joke and..."

"Stop it," said Tots, holding her ears, "you're just being mean because I didn't eat your stupid fruit. I own my stories and my name, you can't take them, they belong to me."

"How can a story belong to anyone?" said Darcee, "we share language and if you tell me something I can tell Mum any time I want."

"You dobber," said Tots, "you derivative dobber maths booboornarring!"

"Don't talk ingenious with me," said Darcee, "you'll upset Otto, I think he's very keen on the ingenious."

And Tots started to cry and she wept, throbbing on her desk, and she looked particularly boiling and scalded, worse than if her parents had been disappointed.

"I thought you were my big sister," she said, muffled by herself, "but all you want to do is make fun of me because of Otto; and I thought I was Otto! You're... you're... you're MEAN!"

"Come on Otto," said Darcee to her friend from Imagination, "you say you've got a lot of friends my age, but you want to marry me. You are friends with a lot of children. But you want to marry me. I am so special, aren't I, Tots? Oh, that's right, you're not talking to me because you're a baby; well, come on Otto."

And Darcee left arm in air with Otto and Tots kept crying until they were well out of earshot.

She lifted one arm, so she could see out with an eye, then the other arm, and realised she was free from pain.

She had the fruit still there, and her tears that clung to her hot cheeks made her feel cold and clammy even though she was very boiling still from rage and banshee-weep.

"I'm going to make my own friend FROM imagination," said Tots, "and I'm not going to eat my fruit, I am going to imitate it and be inspired by it; I am going to hope by looking at it."

"Are you sure that's the right thing to do, little one?" said a voice.

Tots got a fright. She kept it mostly in her heart, which leapt like salt and tang and static from a swing or pram.

She looked around, but there was no one there.

"I'm not sure what that was," she said to herself and not to no-one-someone, "but I'm going to make up my imaginary friend in my story, inspired by the please-please-please look of this weird fruit."

She began to write on her big blank page in orange crayon thicker than her fingers:

BIG FRUIT NAM

Then she crossed it out

~~BIG FRUIT NAM~~

"That's not write," she said.

BIG FRUIT MAN

"That's better," she said, "but not what I want. I'm a little girl, and I don't want a big man. I've never met a boy before, and Otto is Darcee's invisible friend, and I don't know who that voice was before. I want a little boy, a little boy like me, like me and like my age who likes me and wants to take time with me."

She wrote something else:

LOVEHEART LITTLE BOY

THE FRUIT BOY

"My sister is busy with her invisible Otto, and has left me in the chilly," said Tots, "well, maybe if I imagine my Loveheart Little Boy... the Fruit Boy, then I'll have company too. Maybe my sister will love me again, but for now I'll have to make do with my Loveheart Little Boy in my happy story, because I want to be happy. Happy is super duper for little girls."

And saying that made her feel happy. And she giggled.

"What can Loveheart Little Boy do, I wonder?"

She looked at the fruit, and as if copying something from it drew a stick figure of a little boy with a shaved head in a garden.

"Yeah," she said to what she had drawn, "aren't you cute. Cutie cutie old boy, little boy. Yeah, you're a big vootie cutie! "

And she drew herself next to him, in a thinner pink crayon, in a frilly dress made of a line of loops like ribbons for helping the door of the poor; and she was maybe a tad shorter than he was.

"And we're going to have picture adventures," she said.

She looked at the fruit and frowned.

"You're trouble, fruit thing," she said to it, "I'm going to graft you back onto the tree where Darcee found you before she got engaged in Otto-Toilet! Otto Poopoo. Doodoo Oopoopoo! Booooooo!"

So she took the big fruit and walked back to where the tree was.

"I don't know gardening," she said, "Loveheart Little Boy does, but he's just a story right now. I've got to hope and be my goal as a girl if I am to hope him into my heart. I've got to put this inspiration back where I found it, so Mum and Dad can see I'm a good girl and I don't steal things like my lubby sissy Darcee who just made a bad mistake. I miss her so much already. How many hours has it been. I think it's been 139! I'm sure it has. It's almost lunch since breakfast."

She found a stalk of a leaf, and tied the stub of the stalk from the fruit back together, a sort of weave, like a braid, or rope, or twine, or chain.

"That'll do," she said.

And before her eyes, a shimmer of gold came down and the fruit grafted back on the tree.

"Wow," she said, "Loveheart Little Boy is going to be so proud of me as his best friend, I am SO good at gardening."

And then, before her eyes, lights like red and white and blue came from the roots of the tree, and the tree rose up, and the branches all swirled around like a sea aenenome, but friendly and not creepy at all. Just like a happy thing, not like something eerie like a bed monster or closet monster or space eater.

"Goodbye tree," said Tots, waving into the sky, "you can have your apple sauce back because I used it without using it. I'm a good girl."

7:32PM

4: Morning Dins (Anna And Redorthy)

Written: March 26th 2020 ace (begun 7:48PM)

Tabula was outside playing ping pong with a cork table tennis racquet and a rubber ball on a bit of elastic. She was waitng for Mum to come home with some carob. She was getting carob because that was healthy, and Tots was trying to try to get used to trying new things.

"I can get ten bounces, I bet," she said, and got to three rebounds and the ball fell off the paddle.

And then, a couple walked by, and stopped to say hello. Two adults, young man and woman, hand in hand.

"Hello," they said, "is your mother at home?"

"No, she is out," said Tots, feeling even smaller than her namesake, "Dad is in the back working on his uniform for work. It's all the same colour because that's what a uniform means. That's what Dad says."

"He's good with words," said the man, "Hi, my name's Redorthy."

She shook his hand, it felt like clay. A bit sweaty. She was a bit scared.

"It's good to know someone like this man in this wide brown land," said the woman, "he's my fiance."

"Is that like a white aeroplane?" asked Tots.

"Well, no." said the woman. "It's more like a boyfriend who wants to be your husband and keeps saying he will in a promise."

"Oh, that's lovely," said Tots, small and sad but brave.

She put her paddle down.

"What's your name?" Tots asked the lady.

"I am Anna Batiste," said the lady, "and we live in a garden a little way away."

"It's hard to work it all by yourself." said Redorthy.

"I bet," said Toto.

"But I help," said Anna, "but I keep getting dirty and I need lots of baths. It's not right to be dirty all the time when sometimes you can look beautiful. That's right, to look beautiful."

Toto Tabula Rosa smiled.

"Am I beautiful?" she asked.

"You're lovely," said Anna, reaching down and tenderly holding Tot's right hand, "and you can be a gardener too."

"I am a gardener," said Tots, suddenly more excited that 100 years of red cordial, "I had a fruit-and-wrote-a-story-about-loveheart-little-boy-and-then-I-had-aninspirefruitandthe fruit went on the tree and... and... and..."

"And that's lovely," said Anna, "you can show us how to help trees like that make lots of fruit for everyone to enjoy."

"And you don't need to eat fruit to enjoy it?" said Tots, pleadingly almost.

"Yes, that's right," said Redorthy, "farmers grow lots of fruit they don't eat, and it feeds families, and then they get silver coins to obtain other things they need for their own family."

"Like crayons and paper?"

"That's the idea," said Redorthy, "and chairs and doors, and carpet, and carpentry, and cutlery, and electricity, sometimes phones..."

"Wow, all that from growing lots of fruits trees?"

"Yes," said Anna, "isn't it amazing, to be a gardener family?"

"It sounds wonderful," said Tots, "I'm sure Loveheart Little Boy would love it."

"Is that your special friend?" asked Redorthy, grinning.

"No, he's just a story," said Tots, looking glum, "but I hope I meet a boy just like him one day and we can be gardener best friends forever and ever and ever and we can learn everything together. I want my sister to visit too, and even Otto can come if he's polite..."

Tots clung to Redorthy's leg.

"Can you be my uncle?" she asked.

"Okay," he said, "I'll be Uncle Red, okay?"

"Oh, wow!" said Tots, and ran around arms out like a crazy aeroplane from the golden age of ballooning, "I've got an uncle!"

"Oh hi," said Bushranger Rosa, stepping out of his terrace front door, "are you two new here? I see Tots has given you a great welcome. She loves being like a mat, you know?"

"I love my new uncle, Dad," said Tots.

"Redorthy Swawod," said the man, shaking Dad's hand.

"Anna Batiste," said Anna, smiling politely.

"Ah yes," said Dad, stroking his chin, "I recognise that name, but I'll keep it discreet, k?"

"No worries, mate," said Redorthy, "say, do you have wheelbarrow?"

"One to spare," said Dad, "you want it?"

"Wonderful," said Uncle Red, "we'll come for it tomorrow."

"Bless the pair of you," said Dad, and as they walked off hand in hand he said.

"What a lovely couple."

And Tots watched them go, thoughtfully and without a fully concluded smile or frown, just a thoughtful medi'm.

8:08PM

5: Weapons Of Nightmares

Written: 26th-27th March 2020 (begun 11:43PM on the 26th)

Tots went to sleep that night and dreamt a dream;

She was in a palm estuary and there were large green pineapples the size of cafes.

And there was a neon sign that read:

SAFE

And she tried to get to it; but there was something not very nice in the way;

It was a bad thing; a bad thing made of clear plastic, shaped like a person a little taller than her, a bit tubby, and full of wee wee;

"Me Chambh," it said, "wee wee runs the world; you will grow and drink beer and think all books are about wee wee."

"LEAVE HER ALONE," came a familiar voice, and Tots woke up in her bed.

Night was scary after a bad dream like that and she didn't want to go to the toilet at all. What if there were bats, or bullants, or spiders, or shadows dark that you could feel them, or if she got thirsty in the toilet and she ran dry? All these horrible things?

What if there was the Chambh Monster?

Shivering and slowly pulling her well crafted embroidered patterned blanket up; which felt coarse as a mountain beggar's coat after that; she looked around her room.

On her bedside, there was a book she had never seen before.

It was big, thin and had a beautiful picture on the front, by a master painter.

It was her, her and a man with wooly white hair.

And the book said on word on the front:

TODAY

And it said the author

BY SAINT LITTLEBOX WAITALOT

"I like reading," she said to herself, and she was too afraid to even think about her stores now that she'd written herself, "I can turn my night light on just enough..."

And she did so, and the room glowed green but comforting like overhugging trees with nice leafy shadow, like a summer's day and it's like night wasn't even there; but it wasn't blinding and it's not like rest had turned away from her that she would be cranky later;

She picked up the book gradually, making sure she wouldn't get a papercut from the clean, crisp paper which was treated, somehow recycled, but new, odd but it's not like she'd had much experience with paper making; she was still getting used to paperbark on trees when her Bushranger Father would take her out on a daddy daughter date.

The man with the wooly hair was friendly; he looked like a sheep a bit; but a sheep who wasn't scared or jumpy; just one that would let you give him a big hug; but a sheep that liked reading.

"A sheep that liked reading," said Tots to herself, very softly.

She opened the page.

This is a book about a Sheep that Liked Reading but Never Went To School; and this book is the easiest way for you, Rosy Tot, to understand all the things he wrote in the world; and he wrote libraries of books; but first you must learn to read; Tabula!

"I know how to read," said Tots, decidedly, carefully but very gently, like pressing a rubber stamp to a page and not wanting to smudge.

What story would you like to read first?

"Oh, I get to pick," said Tots, like a note to self slightly, softly edgily, "what shall I like to read first? I'd like to know how not to be scared of Chambh Monsters full of Wee Wee and made of plastic. Because that will help me if I ever, ever have that awful dream again."

Do not fear; I am with you; I want to tell you a story, Rosy Tot;

I want to tell you a story about how I met some people who tried to trap me with words;

And you may think it's funny that a word can trap you;

Why, a word is a sound that comes out of your mouth;

Can you imagine a whole country being defeated by a burp?

Or a war ended by a hiccup?

Even if you can imagine these things, you will be safe, Rosy Rosa.

When I lived in the Land;

A Good Land; a land of Four Dirts;

Some Dirts good for gardens;

And some Very Old;

Some Very Worn;

And some Not Deep;

When I live THERE;

Then men came to me;

And they were men who were pretending to be not pretending;

You know what it's like to pretend: you're a little girl;

But if you pretend that you're not pretending and you're REALLY pretending;

That gets lots of people confused;

Imagine if you were Princess and you were pretending that you're not pretending

And you REALLY were pretending;

It's very confusing for the people;

Who want to have their bread and their cordial and time to play after gardening;

Many men were good men

Many men wrote and read good books

Many men and women were actors who entertained and comforted

And gave people a good day off because they had worked hard

But some men

Men who were pretending they were not pretending but really were pretending;

I was angry at them

Because they confuse the children

And they were a lot like Chambh

They said they wanted to protect the Land

But they really were only interested in

Wee Wee

Let's no go there;

But they tired me out

And tried me with tests

And tested me with trials

And asked me questions

To see if I would pretend their pretend-I'm-not-pretending-but-I'm-really-pretending game

But I knew how to diffuse their mock bomb

And I gave them water to drink

Water of words

That made them think

Don't go to war aganst Chambh monsters;

Use your words!

Words are powerful!

Words let people know you are for real;

Words are the first point of call;

That means you look to your Word first

Remember; You are a little one;

Who needs your Mum and your Dad

And even your sister Darcee

Don't worry about Otto

Sometimes we have weird phases

When we grow up, weird things happen

But we get through

And though there is wee wee

We stop thinking about it all the time

And this is what we call

Not being

CONSPICUOUS

That's a big work, a big work to read a big word;

And there are many words for big that are big to describe big words

Like MONUMENTAL and GARGANTUAN and EPIC; wait... that's a little word!

Sometimes there are surprises that even I don't know;

But you don't know how much one is supposed to know that I know;

You have only just met me; a moment ago;

And now you are closer to being in the know;

How do you do, Toto?

And Toto smiled; and a little tear ran down her cheek because it was the last of the fear from her monster nightmare; and energy came back to her little heart.

And always say Grace after every meal

Because with Grace, you can try things
Grace means you can try
And it's okay if you have a go
Even if you make a little mess
You are learning
You can try hot food
You can try cold food
You can try sweet food
You can try salty food
You can try solid food
You can try ice-cream
But that's pretty effortless, hey?
And Grace at dinner means thanks;
It is saying "isn't it nice to have good food,
I am not sure how it all got here.
So many ingredients, from all over the world
And it's here, on my table.
Thanks One and All!"
Goodnight, Toto Tabula Rosa, my little daughter of this Book;

And Tabula smiled a smile, and though she wasn't crying anymore, her eyes softened, and she didn't seem so intent. And she rested back on her pillow, the nightlight watching over her, and she fell back asleep and forgotten even the name of that monster.

What was it? Bloop? Blepo? Bunto? Bobo?

Doesn't matter; it's no longer on the grid, Rosy Tot.

We don't measure it anymore.

We've outgrown it.

Time for better things.

Next chapter.

(Finished: 12:18AM; 27th March 2020 ace)

6: Waiting For... And Something Unexpected

Written: 27th March 2020 (begun 9:53AM)

Redorthy was going through his garden while Anna Batiste his fiance had a bath.

And there, in the midst of his garden, was a tree he'd never seen before.

Can you guess which tree it was?

It was the tree that had been in the Rosa's yard, the one whose twin fruit Darcee had eaten from and Tots had been inspired by and put back. The one whose roots had just picked up and flown away; a very unorthdox tree, you might say, but a very jolly one.

"Hello," said Redorthy, examining the leaves.

It took him what Anna would have called an unreasonable amount of time to find that fruit that Tabula had grafted back on, but he found it.

It had grown a bit, so now it was the size of a watermelon, like a watermelon with soft limbs, two arms, two legs, and it was pink with a tinge of green that no one would have mentioned, but in memory later would have been aware of.

Redorthy looked in wonder.

"Aren't you a lucky one?" he said, "Not many fruits are as unique as you are, son."

Now he said son, because that's just a lovely way of acknowledging something; even royalty talks to plants in such a way; but Redorthy was more true in his aphorisms that he'd care to confess.

And then, the heavy fruit fell from the tree and into a great pile of leaf litter Redorthy had gathered together, leaves of brown and crackerlyness. Runch, runch, runch, and they comforted the little Fruit

Boy like a hug, like a soft place to fall, because they were a soft place to fall.

"Hey," said Redorthy, a bit gruffly, and then more gentle, like a whisper, "hey."

And then he could see, looking into the pile, that it was a child. A smiling, happy child; a child that wanted to learn; a toddler; a tot the age of Miss Rosa, and a year younger than her sister Darcee.

And Redorthy was a simple man, he wasn't the best at reading. He would have realised that there were markings on the tree like instructions about what had happened and why the fruit had become a child, and we would have a much more filled out story; but that's not how it went down; we can't understand everything, because we as a people aren't focusing on everything all the time.

So Redorthy picked up the child, wrapped him in a banana leaf and gave him a blessing:

"God Offers Health, Mate," he said, "God Offers Health, Mate, and a good home. Go home, and you'll be coming to me and Anna, okay? Gone fishin'? Not me, Mate. You're going to be okay with us."

He looked at the little infant, with his shaved head, seemingly shaved. Redorthy hadn't pruned the tree or its fruit, and G.O.H.M. (as his parents would call him, short for "God Offers Health, Mate") was quite well developed that even his head looked like it had been pampered for a handsome pageant; I guess that's what you would have called it.

Gohm was blessed, and every time his parents called his name he'd get a blessing again.

And this was very unusual in the town of Boone Readimus; for most people had a nice nickname and usually a very rude real name, the fathers more frequently than the ladies.

But who knew the meaning of Gohm's name apart from his two parents?

Would you have guessed it?

Not I at first glance, that's for sure.

(Finished 27th March 2020, 10:09AM)

7:Darcee's Nap

(Written 27th March 2020; started 10:16AM)

Darcee was napping in the afternoon while Tots was in the sun, in the sandpit, with her straw hat on playing sandcastles.

She had a dream of that nasty monster that Tots had had. Let's not mention his name.

And he looked at Darcee.

"Boo!" he said.

And the boy Otto came to the girl's rescue, just as Darcee had pictured him in her everyday imagination, in a green outfit and with a big smile and a leaf.

And Otto tickled the monster with the leaf, and all that the monster was went clear and leaked out and evaporated.

"No more monster," said the dream boy, "no more worries, and no more me."

"No more you, Ot?" asked Darcee, very concerned, "that's not nice, I caught you from eating the tree."

"Yes, but you must be nice to your sister," said Ot, "there are dream people more bigger in niceness that know me;"

"You're very nice, Otto," said Darcee, "come sit down and we'll have tea from our teaset."

"Will you remember me, Darcee?" asked Otto.

"I can write a story about you," said Darcee.

"Sis is better at that," said Otto, "you could try, but I think, from the high high place, that Orders say that you'd best bake a cake to remember me by instead."

"A cake!" Darcee gasped. "Wow, a cake! I've baked biscuits before but never a whole cake. I'm going to need Mother Rosa's help."

"That's okay," said Otto, "I'm imaginary, I'm every child's imaginary friend, and sometimes even **I** need help."

"You weren't everyone's imaginary friend..." said Darcee softly, "not Tot's."

"Yes, that is odd isn't it?" said Otto, sitting down next to Darcee on the bed, sitting up as she did, "she never had an imaginary friend, and yet she imagines A LOT. What would you call that?"

"I'd call that my sister," smirked Darcee.

And then she woke up, and Otto was vanished and unsummonable.

"Goodbye, Otto." whispered Darcee, and went to get a glass of water from the bathroom, the sink by the shower and bath.

There was a plastic cup for both her and her sister.

Hers was sky blue and Tab's was pink, like pink ink.

Mother Rosa came over as Darc' was having her clear drink.

"What would like to do this afternoon?" asked her mother.

"I wanna bake a cake in memory of Otto," said Darcee.

"Has Otto moved on?" asked her mother, "I wonder where he went?"

10:29AM

The Letters Of Tabula

12th - 14th January 2020

Contents:

Bushranger Rosa's Love For His Daughter Toto Tabula

Tabula To Daddy Rosa

Deep Water In The Billy

Trust And Uber

A Lullaby For The Bushranger

Cool Oceans

Jesser's Dresser

Spill Derbins

Green Days

Rosebird

Bushranger Rosa's Love For His Daughter Toto Tabula

12th January 2020

So we are here, dear, we are here, and do not fear cause we are here. And we love you, me and Mum. We love you very much. And we are so, so, so, so, sad you get so sick sometimes. And we sit by your bed and we wonder what the matter is with you. And sometimes I get angry, but it's not a hard anger or a burning anger, its much more mellow, like a white rose of the heart, and love is like that.

I may have my armour as a Bushranger, wandering from Bottlebrush Hollow all the way as far as Alumriance in the north, but my heart is very soft for you, my beautiful, beautiful Tabs. You and Darcee are my best friends in a lot of ways. No, I wouldn't let you get away with what me and my friends did when we were young, but I love listening to you. I could listen to you for a million years. I could sit and yarn for a thousand patchwork quilts. And though I try to sew, that's not it, because you make my laugh so much, my darling daughter, you have me in stitches.

When you read that book, that one you don't like showing me, please don't be shy. Since you've been reading it, you become kinder, and gentler, peace and you know how to manage your temper better. And you seem to be a lot more controlled about all your fairy tale romance meanderings. You could give me a squiz once in a while. A girl with a library like hers in her room, like a great garden, should not be ashamed of her books. Not of a single journal, not of a single article of news. Got it?

And while we're on the subject of romance, what do you think of that boy Gohm? He's very funny, I don't think he's worked out that you don't need to work everything out.

Please be gentle with him, Toto. Please be incredibly gentle with him. Boys like that have very soft hearts. A lot of boys will take you for a ride and lie to you. See, Gohmo though, he needs to realise that he just has to let go and he will see for miles.

I see your mother wants to change your curtains. What do I know about curtains, Tabula! You talk about curtains with golden box behind them.

What do you want for your birthday, Tabs? It's coming up. Yes, I know you'd like to be married, but you're a bit too young yet. Come on, what else can I give you. I suppose I could give you a toy.

Not really into toys, though, are you Tab?

It's a town I'd rather have as a better town, this one. It's a good base to leave from, because if I was in a really comfortable town it would be hard to leave and do my job. And that is just like a half cold cup of coffee with milk in, isn't it? Sink that one. Ew-wee.

Nice to catch up. I'll see you when I get home from Sweepe.

Muchos lovabos,

Dad xx

Tabula To Daddy Rosa

13th January 2020

Hi Daddy,

I'm all right at the moment. I don't know why I have a hot water bottle. It is very capricious. It's a bit like that cold cup of coffee you said.

I don't think I could drink coffee from a hot water bottle though, I think things have to be the right thing in the right place.

In that place that I read about with the curtains and the golden box, there were a lot of things in the right place. But I think there was a man who was going to be king who put things out of order. He took some bread he wasn't supposed to because his soldiers were hungry. But things were out of order anyway. They said he would be king, but another man was king, and he wouldn't be king because they said that that man was already king.

What do you do, Daddy, when you're told two different things, and they're both true, but you wonder how they can be both true at the same time?

Me and Darc', we're sisters. And we're both true, but we're different things at the same time.

What would I like for my birthday? I'd like it to be Christmas at the same time as my birthday. We could have two calendars that say different things in the same room and we could just sit there and eat marinated chicken.

I do like toys, but I like dreaming of stories about toys rather than playing with toys. I guess because in your head more things are variable. And its easier to say sorry and start the whole thing over.

But it's not really a mistake to imagine the thing you don't like when deciding what you quite like, is it, Daddy?

I'm glad you like me, it makes me feel much better in my heart. :)

I like my book very much that I read the most. Because there's someone I found that I can talk to. He helps me be better in my heart too. He helps me understand Gohm because he was a boy once too who had it a bit tricky.

Gohm is okay. I can just settle with him like snow on the ground. We can just sit there in the garden, like two snowflakes in a winter's drift.

And what I'd like to know is do snowflakes become more alike in the spring?

You've got a very big beard, and that makes you seem important. But you're very silly, Daddy.

Love ya,

Tabby.

Deep Water In The Billy

13th January 2020

Well, Tabby!

You can imagine a bad thing, a thing of bad taste. Knowing what you prefer and not is how you pick a favourite. Sometimes it takes a little while. Sometimes there's patience involved.

You've got to know you're favourite flavour of ice-cream though! Lose that, and you lose your soul.

What's the point if you own all the ice cream shops in the world, but you don't have that special cone you always like when you feel blue?

And what would you trade in exchange for that favourite ice cream? Nothing, that 2 dollar bill you paid the ice-cream man ripped him off, right?

You see, you could imagine a marinated chicken flavoured ice-cream. You could imagine it just long enough to know that that's absolutely foul, and then discard it. And you'll then have the conclusion that you don't like it and nothing more.

Does that someone you talk to from your book say the same things as me. Or I suppose he likes gelato rather than ice-cream?

What's the difference between gelato and ice-cream... I know how you think, Tabs, you're going to ask me that.

Ice-cream is made from milk, and gelato is water based.

Gelato is probably more like a snowflake, so I guess you and Gohmmo are like a couple of scoops of gelato, in a twin cone.

I like that idea better than you and him just sitting in some garden waiting for the spring. You've got to be poetic, Tabs. Don't mix your metaphors.

Well, you can if you want, but not in front of the mayor.

I hardly think a hot water bottle is capricious. A hot water bottle is your friend, Tabula. It's not going to crawl away like a slug and leave you cold!

Does my beard make me seem important... I think I fit in better with nature with a beard. I could go without it one day and wig you out a bit. Yeah, I could even make it into a wig. You'd wear it, wouldn't you? I think you'd be a most venerable beard-head. :p

Christmas is a historical event. And your birthday is too.

As for paradoxes, let them quack for a bit, and then they can fly off together and make a nest later. Contradictions often attract each other, Tabula.

Kings and mayors and luncheons...

Love,

Your Bushranger Dad

I'm So Glad I'm Not In Trouble

13th January 2020

Hi Daddy,

Maybe Gohm can wear your beard on his face. That's much more orderly. And it's more family, because then he inherits from you and he's really like close to us.

Ice-cream would be hard to inherit though, wouldn't it, Daddy? Because it melts. Like you can't even bring me an ice-cream from Sweepe. Are you still in Sweepe? Where are you now?

Have you seen any nice animals?

Some parents around here say that nice is a boring word, but I don't see why. It makes me comfortable and just saying it makes me feel so much better. Better than my proxy friend hot water bottle.

Do you think of me as a duck? Because, maybe. But then I think that Darcee is my sister, and I don't think of her as a duck. I just think of her as someone very human. Ducks don't make very good soup, I mean they don't sit over a big pot with a ladle and make celery and onion and bouyabaisse and all that stuff.

If me and Gohm are gelato, I wonder what flavour we are? Whether we are the same flavour or a different flavour?

Do you think it's romantic if a boyfriend and girlfriend like the same ice-cream? Because it's nice to match, but then you can't try each other's flavour and discover new things.

I don't think Gohm is ready for me to share any ice-cream with him. But I suppose he might eat a few chips that were left over from dinner with me, provided that they were in a separate bowl that was practically public.

I don't think Gohm would call me his girlfriend yet, either.

I don't like thinking in detail about manky things. Like, not even a hint of that. Like, the name is enough, marinated chicken ice-cream. No, don't even say the name in full, Daddy! I get the idea and I don't like it. I don't need to read a bad story in full to conclude that I don't like it.

Darcee, as a bit of a chef, talks about an accquired taste. Can you imagine that, putting a taste into your backpack and walking around with it? Collecting tastes?

Poetry is okay, like I like rhymes. I like meter. Poetry without rhyme and meter is too much like Franchiska Arrows. You see her at her gallery, and its like she's already decided that she's in heaven.

Spring is beautiful, Daddy. It's the best season ever.

You want to see me mix my metaphors?

Giving away secrets is like looking a gift charlie horse in the hospital full of apples, and there's no doctors.

Now I've got a headache, you were right Daddy, bad to mix silly-mes and meddle-fauxs.

And now, alas! My punishment is more than I can bear!

I love you so much!

Toto

Trust And Uber

13th January 2020

Hi Tabula,

If Gohm wore my beard, do you think his fathers would like that? Because then he could boss them round for a change.

But no, I don't believe in insubordination. Rebellion sounds great, but then you realise if water rebelled plumbing we'd have nothing in the tap. If ovens rebelled, all our food would be cold. If vegetables rebelled, they wouldn't grow and they'd be all manky. Have you seen a bad bunch of carrots? It's not pretty, Tabs.

And when something rebels, how do you put it right? Well, when you do something wrong, I correct you, don't I? But I haven't needed to do that much now that you're reading that book and have that friend.

And I know you worry, and you say that Darcee says that you don't do as many bad things because you're mostly in bed and you don't really have a chance to get in trouble. Aye, there's always critics. Siblings always do that.

Food is temporary. New wave after new wave.

I left Sweepe a little while ago, hun. I'm now going through a lot of red deserts, and there's lots of good fellers to talk to, and we have a good laugh and we sit and just talk for hours and hours. There's not as many plants to look after, but these fellers know where everything is, every leaf and every lizard and ant and everything.

I'd like to know about you that much, and I try as your Dad, but, Tabula, you always surprise me. You always do. I really love you.

Nice is a great word. They're great biscuits to go with your coffee. Better than calling tea biscuits "escargoteric" or something like that. You can put that in your bin dictionary. Whoop!

I quite think of Darcee as a duck a whole lot, Tabs. Just like you. She's like a very mother duck. She's your sister, but she really looks after you and is always bring you just what you need. She brings so much warmth into the place. And you have a very tender heart, Tabula. You need someone to stir it up in you.

I think take one day at time with Gohm, little lady. Don't speculate because you'll make a spectacle of yourself, and it will magnify the situation and everyone will see what might just have been a stolen kiss.

Funny that they call them that. Because its something you give, right?

I like your writing, but you like reading a bit better, don't you? You are quick to listen and slow to speak, it's very lovely.

Me? I'll talk your ear right off and your mother will have to stick it back on with glue.

And I've run my quill, and now I say:

Say a prayer for me.
I thought you'd like that, Tabs.
Still trying to figure you out.
But I love you so much.
Dad. x

A Lullaby For The Bushranger

14th January 2020

Daddy:

I think Gohm likes our family best, but he can't say that too loud. Cause there's a crowd around him all the time. I think sometimes when he's with me it's his quiet place. I don't think he's had that much.

I believe in miracles, Daddy. I believe that things can happen, but its not rebellion. If water was needed to a thirsty person, and the pipe was in the ground, and the water stopped its journey and burst out onto the path where they were... I don't think that's rebellion at all.

And the difference between a good carrot and a bad carrot is lots of water. Gohm would know better, he knows gardening more than me.

If a miracle goes wrong... can that happen? Ooh, I'm getting all burbly thinking of that. Why would something so beautiful go so wrong?

But a baby is a miracle, and sometimes they are... well, a mummy and daddy want them to be perfect. Ten fingers, ten toes, all that.

Gohm was perfect, but then someone hurt him, and now he needs help. I love being his miracle, Daddy. He's just a good boy.

I'm kind of asleep to bad things, and alive to my books and my friend. Like, all that bad stuff when I was younger is asleep, and I am alive inside to loving people and doing good things. Because my friend, he's in my heart. Even when I am in bed, and I can dream and its okay.

And the difference between my friend and Gohm, well...

Darcee is nice to me. She just likes to bump me around. But that's what she does. She's my beautiful sister.

It's good to know things in nature, and I'm glad you have someone to talk to. I suppose when you're out in the desert with no one around and you see a feller to talk to you are like crying for joy on the inside and you watch them come up in the steam, all wriggly in the heat and they walk up with what they have in their hands.

Do they shake their hand with you? Do they hug you? How do you introduce yourself to one of these fellers? Do you need to introduce the introduction? What do you do?

I'm just glad you protect me, Daddy. You can stand outside my door, and you can know I'm safe. That's like better than any encyclopedia about me. Just know that I am safe when you protect me, Dad Rosa.

Nice biscuits are good, but I like Monte Carlos the best. It's that icing that isn't quite pink and it isn't quite white, and it so hard to unglue. So you've got to eat it all, but even then. Is it one biscuit or two? That's what I want to noo.

I think that eskapopolis word you just came up with is really horrid.

Darcee the ducky. Well, that makes sense when you spell it out for me. We ducks have to stick together, cause that's what they do. They all sit together by the lake and eat bits of broken bread.

But what do ducks drink? Lake water? I've never seen that, and it's hard for me to dream of that, because they swim in it. It's like drinking bath water. There's water that washes clean and water you drink. But when does one become the other?

If I had asked, I could get some water. In a lot of ways.

Darcee is always filling up a pitcher for me and I have my little pink cup by my bed, by my sky blue alarm clock. But I can't say I use my alarm clock much. It is very noisy, Daddy.

Gohm has kissed my hand. He gave it to me, but I gave my hand to him. Darcee was the only one who saw. And my pink cup was there, but that's plastic and not glass and nothing like a spectacle.

Monocles are for rich people, but it's good to have two eyes. Gohm has the cube which he sees with. But he is rich because he has a family like us to go to when he feels sad.

And he doesn't always show that he's sad. He's just happy to see me and he wants to forget all the others stuff. But sometimes you just have to say things aren't right at home, even when you're in a nice place away from it and don't want to wreck it.

I do like writing better when I write to you, Daddy.

I don't think you could talk my ear off! My hair will protect me, you know I like to have it over my ears.

I can pray for you, Daddy. But I don't want to use pen and ink. That's what the Elder says.

The Elder is a very loving man who wants kids to stay away from idols.

I don't know what an idol is really, but it's really upsetting when someone is married and there is an idol around.

That's all I know, I've been a bit giddy but I'd like to do more reading.

Don't try to figure me out, Daddy. I am not maths, I am a little girl. And maths can't give you cuddles when you get home.

"Oh, look! I am the grand and pompous 3.2,

And I love you, Boshranga!"

No, I don't think it works like that at all!

Love:

T. T. Rosa

Cool Oceans

14th January 2020

Little Tabby-la-la,

Gohm can prefer us, but we always send him home. He does have to grow up one day. He is their ward, and he makes them better just as much as they raise him up to be something.

Your room is very quiet, Tabula. It's like there is a peace ghost in there and it makes it all restful and calm.

Do you believe in peace ghosts? I hadn't really thought of it, myself. I don't think they'd be the sort of thing that would have a name, or they wouldn't introduce themselves by name too much.

And here I am speculating. But it's only because of evidence. And it's evident that you are in a very restful place. I can protect you very easy, kid, when there's that kind of peace in the room. Love ya.

Wait, I don't say that til the end of the letter. No, I have to address your other wonderous remarks, don't I? Don't let me push off without having another punt!

Might be something going on, maybe the peace ghost tries to make some peace by warning you of things, Tabula. That's what happening up here.

Yeah, the fellers are stirring. Takes a lot to stir them, they know EVERYTHING about this place. Don't worry for me, say your prayers like you do to your friend, and ask for a bit of protection for me from that Peace Ghost.

We'll have bags of time together when I get home:

Bushrosa.

Jesser's Dresser

14th January 2020

Daddy,

I hope you're okay. That sounds spooky, like a cat on a hot dime roof.

I prayed you'd be okay. So I know you will be. Like leaning on my bed and being sure I'm not going to fall on the ground and spill my water and cry.

But I almost feel like crying. I hope you're okay. Daddy

Tabby

Spill Derbins

14th January 2020

Dear Tabs,

It all turned out okay.

Moved on now. In some in between place, a lot of shifting things and sands and this and that. You need to look for a rock in a place like this. All else is just... what would you call it? Transitory?

I've got a joke for you:

Why did the melon eat the bank?

I don't have an answer given in my own words. But what do you think?

Dad

Green Days

14th January 2020

Daddy, I'm so glad you're okay.

I don't know why the melon ate the bank. Because then a melon would be a chest. Full of treasure, kind of blessed. And is this a melon like a person's face?

I know about a hut in a field of melons. That's like in bad times. I'm so glad you're out of bad times, Daddy.

It hurts a bit, because I'm worried. It's painful to keep writing, but I really want to tell you all I can because I want to see you again very much. Darcee is very patient with me. Sometimes I get very feverish. I want to tell you as much as I can.

Sometimes all I can think about is this room. Like I try to open a book, but it's not an escape very far away. And Gohm doesn't always come over when I want him to, and I want to contact him. I wish there were still trumpets for blowing on.

Because he listens to me.

I get very sad, Daddy. Sometimes I'm afraid to tell you. I know you want to protect me, but how can you protect me from my own tears?

You can hug me, and kiss me, but my tears are still in my eyes.

Do you think feelings can make you sick?

I don't think it's germs. I don't think it's ever been germs at all, Daddy.

When you're in trouble, I want to protect you. I want to be sure you're okay. You're so far away.

Please come home. Please.

I'd love a normal day with you, maybe go camping. We could eat all sorts of nice things, and invite Gohm and have a great party. We could go for ages and ages and ages. That would be so much fun.

Sweat isn't sad. Fever is war. Fever is battle.

But tears, tears are because of love.

It's really nice outside. All and everywhere.

I can't wait to see you again.

Love you, love you, love you

xxxxxxxxx

Rosa Tabula

Rosebird

14th January 2020

Dear daughter,

Little Tabs, I never knew you were this sad.

What's up? Why do you feel like that. It hurts very much that a hug or a kiss won't make all your tears go away.

I could make you cocoa, I could make you a bacon sandwich.

I know that's pretty festy, but it's something I know how to make without your mother's help.

Isn't it funny how tomato sauce cooks different when a father makes something compared to a mother? Well, that's what I find anyway. Even the cheese on a pita pizza cooks differently.

With me it's so much darker, your Mum is much more tender with cheese. Like, it looks more authentic like it belongs in a restaurant you might have a date in.

I'm trying, Tabula.

I'm going to be home in 3 days. I really want to help you. I have always wanted to see you out and playing with the other kids, and have that special someone you've always wanted for as long as you've known how to talk.

We love you, we all love you, you know that, don't ya?

Sometimes I write poems, so I wrote this one for you on the fly:

Soft little rose,
Soft little rosebird,
Grew from my nest,
And got so high,
Like a heart in love,

Othniel Poole

Embraced by the rib of the chest.
Such a treasure, my girl;
Such a holy delight.
I want you well with all my might!
With all my strength and all my gruff,
Of this fever I've had enough!
Be at peace when you rest,
And by that friend of yours,
Who to your inner eyes,
Opens so many of your deep, deep doors,
May you rise from that soft bed,
And all the continent,
Will rise and give applause!
And when you rise,
We will get you such a treat!
Such a big picnic of food,
Anything you'd like to eat!
And you know that I mean it
Dad loves you
3 days, that's it. :")

Darcee Gets An A+

April 23rd - 28th 2020

One:
Silent Tea
April 23rd 2020; 5:36PM

Darcee Rosa was gathering straws in the dust.

"What are you doing that for?" asked Tabs, her sister who had only recently married Gohm Batiste.

"Right back at ya!" said Darc', pointing to Tabula's diamond ring she kept polishing.

When Darcee had been a toddler she had had an imaginary friend called Otto and had even dreamt he had been a Waiter from outer space and even another reality.

That happens in an imaginary relationship; oh lass!

"When am I going to find a nice guy?" said Darcee, resting on a thick corkwood bough. "A real one. One for a Lady."

Two:
Tea First
April 23rd 2020; 5:43PM

Darcee had tea with Tabs and Gohm. Gohm had grown some hot Monatotos that were a special breed of ancient x-perientations.

"I like these, Toby," said Tabula to her mister.

"What ARE they?" asked Darcee.

"Soup veggies," said Gohm Toby.

"And I had them raw," said Tabs, "Gohm, why didn't we boil them?"

"Could I have some to take home?" said Darc'.

"Gohm, go get a paper bag," said Tabs, and she counted fingers, "get three."

"One for each of us," said Darcee, "We'll eat them when I make three unique recipes from each."

"We can all have a bit from each one." said Toby.

Three:
Nanna Rosa
April 23rd 2020; 6:03PM

A letter appeared on Tabula's slate that she kept records of books she had read on:

It was from Nanna Rosa.

Nanna Rosa was in Prison in P'sayz, a town in the reasonably distant north-east.

She was there because she had the wisdom of Talcology de Tor.

"What's that?" asked Darcee

Four:
Mock-Tea
April 23rd 2020; 6:08PM

Tabs and Darcee looked at the Rosatiste Slate, as it was understood in the fam.

And behold, there were words!

Five:
To Do List
April 24th 2020; 12:07PM

Toto Tabula Rosa needed quiet now. She paced two paces, looked at her maroon moccasins and sighed sharply.

"What. Did. Nanna. Rosa. Mean?" she said. "We move to do something decent, if we were boss of prisons we would get her out."

"Benmann could try?" suggested Gohm.

W.C. Benmann was emperor of quite a bit. With will being free often the bless opened to not as much.

"Didn't Othello and Franchiska visit P'sayz?" said Darcee. "And Gohm's worm pals got all over to get the invite to our Thanks Party."

Tabula grated her teeth: evoking a spinster of great age. Gohm Taby Batiste tried not to chuckle.

"You could ring," when he'd gotten his act together that's what Tob' said, "you ring Blepo Asheropolis all the time."

"Blepo isn't wed to Lapwing yet, wingding," said Darcee, banging Gohm in the arm.

Six:
To Get A Call
April 24th 2020; 12:16PM

Because it was a considerably more distant call then Blepo's Parish, Tab Rosa called the switch operator: named Shona Peacehome.

"Hello, Tabby," said Shona, "glad we can talk, even though your aural destination is not I, Shona."

"Yes, you are very funny," said Tabula primly, "but I am wanting a call to P'sayz P'say-Sore Prison to Nanna Rosa."

Shona tapped a few keys on her Amian-274156.12589B which was one of a small handful of personal computers on the great continent of Sootream, where Sweepe, Alisse, Thanks, P'sayz and many other wonderplaced villes were.

"Today she has one Phone Call," said Shona Peacehome, "though you must be sure she wants to spend it on you; keep in mind she sent you a message already."

"Hmm," said Tabula, with a glee.

Seven:
Nanna Says Hi
April 24th 2020; 12:32PM

Shona and Tabs hit the # on their phone at the same time.

"# love," said Tabula, then dialed L. O. V. then E.

And Nanna Rosa picked up the phone.

"Tabby," she said, "I'm so confident in you."

"Hi Nan," said Toto, really stupendously giddily happy, "want to ask you about that symbol on your cor-es-spond-ence."

"You'd like me to sort it out sememe to symbol?" said Nanna. "Okay, it's an invite."

"Really?" said Toto. She was smiling so much that the beaming coloured the EQ of the call.

"What we need to do, To," said Nan, "we need to list a plan get some goals. If you had more goals, you'd have a daughter of your own by now. How long…"

Tabula cut her a new sentence.

"Okay," she founded, "we goal to see you, Nan. It's sad being in bed all day and sad… when can we visit?"

"P'sayz is ages away, luv," said Nan, "even with Ludwig's Chariot."

"We can do it," said Gohm a shot afar off, "Let us try. Let us."

Eight:
Starwyrm
April 24th 2020; 12:41PM

Gohm was looking up at the stars at the eleventh hour. He loved where he lived and he was thinking about how different stars were and what home was like for flying starmedites. Maybe they all held onto their quiet planet to dear life because of the gravity of Benmann's World. He dozed off. Tabula was on the phone to Lappidoth Asheropolis. She said it was diplomacy.

She got that from her aunt Beta-Resh Musica, on her Mother's side. Beta-Resh was kind and tough all at the same time. And her and Darcee used to talk as long, as long as Tabs and Lap were going on now. Gohm sighed.

And then…

"2.487.57.XIVC^2"

And before Gohm was a Star. A Star Shocking as a… well, a corpse. That bad.

A Column of Light.

"What are you?" asked Gohm, calmly.

"I. AM. A. STARWYRM." said the Column-Stellaris.

Nine:
Lapwing's "Twe"
April 24th 2020; 12:52PM

Meanwhile, Tabs was bargaining with Lapwing A.

"She wants you to pop the request, Mister Asheropolis, good shepherd."

"Well, I'm not a player," said Lapwing, "I want to be as honest as I can with Blip-Blop. I don't want to invade her space or eat up her patience."

"She loves you, Ash!" said Tabs, "Sooooo much! Just tell her your whole story and she'll wear your ring."

"It's a bit twee, my story."

"You mean you have a double story?" suggested To.

"No, not the like two, twee like cheese on toast, like saltmite on a crumpet. Like pea soup with mushy peas on the side. Boring!"

"Sometimes plain can take you places," said Tabula, bluntly.

She stopped and looked outside and saw Toby exchanging thought with the Starwyrm. She rolled her eyes and caught the glint of the micro-chandelier in their comm-room.

"Excuse me, pastor, my husband is talking to an alien."

"We are to love the Samaritan." said Pastor Asheropolis, "but you mean a Starwyrm, don't you?"

Tabs sorted her focus, raised her eyebrows and nodded with a grinmace.

"Yes," she decided, "New Jerusalem has let you on the inside track."

Tabula giggled.

"You're not boring at all." and…

Ten:
Benmann
April 24th 2020; 1:07PM

Rivergate and the Brilliant were discussing life.

And this is what they said:

"Shall Toby and Rosa have a child?" said Rivergate. "Is Toby ready?"

"No boy is complete," said the Brilliant.

"Let him hypothesise for a bit," said Rivergate. "Hey?"

"This will be a mare of light," laughed Benmann, Counsellor of Counsellors.

Eleven:
Morning Quiche
April 24th 2020; 1:11PM

In the morning Darcee had made the first of the 3 Monatoto's dishes.

"Quiche," Toto Tabula Rosa cried.

"Protein and Buttie Pie," said Toby.

"No, you know what I call it?" said Darce' above the steam on the blue tartan and oriental plate, "I call it Melotot."

"Wow!" Tabula clapped, "You named it after me."

"You are very mellow, Tab," said Toby, and gave her a taut side-hug.

Twelve:
"12"
April 24th 2020; 1:28PM

Tabula was eating her Melotot next to her sure thing Gohm when in her brain-canvas, that vision place where you are seeing this story, she found herself at a lake talking to Prince of New: W.C. Benmann.

"Hey, hey," said Tabs, "I am here AND I am eating my Melotot. Can you hear that?"

And a sad flute sounded over the lake.

"A pipe sound," said King Benmann, "air goes on a journey and it is a symphonic path."

"Symphonies," said Tabs, "hey, do you think we could sing our way to Nanna Rosa?"

And then Tabs was back next to Gohm with an empty plate.

And he had her arm around her and was smiling.

"Oh, Toby," she said and felt peaceful and gently warm with rest.

Thirteen:
"B"
24th April 2020; 4:14PM

Darcee came with dessert o'the lunch:

"I call them Monatoto with Pototo Tabula Rosettes."

"Darcee!" whined Tabs, "Why do you keep naming things after me?"

"If we had kids we could name them a name too." said Toby.

Tabs punched him, which was still lovely and soft to Gohm, he was decently perceptive like that to her.

"Bit of a B-Dessert," said Tots glumly, she cradled her spoon like civilization was in it.

Fourteen:
Rock Love
24th April 2020; 7:23PM

The following day Darcee was walking south by the coast with ragabond cobbles.

And a young man was going through them examining red rocks and putting them from small to large in a row towards the large gate bollards with the three Great Notches of Fortunate O'No'th.

"They're rocky, aren't they?" said Darcee, grinning from ear to ear.

"They're valuable," said the young man, "the best ones are the loved ones."

He showed a blue stone with chomps, a way around.

"This is an axe head," he said, "someone loved it and used it everyday, a pursuer on trekaround, a way driver and…"

"and the love changes your eyes from geologist to antiquist," grinning on Darcee grinned on.

"Er… yes," said the young man.

"I am Arpelson," said Arpelson the geo-antiquist, "just one name, I am a massive believer in the One."

"Oh, right," said Darcee, wriggling her fingers, and then she picked up a lengthy mauve crystal. "Is this an axe head of heaven?"

"Daft," muttered Arpelson.

"No, Darcee," said D. Rosa.

Fifteen:
This Means Walk And Rosa
24th April 2020; 7:39PM

"So are you local," asked Darcee, as her and Arpelson walked together.

"I am as local as I am where I work, and I am as I is oh so I be," said Arpelson, "see this?"

And the gentlemen showed Darcee a petrified apple.

"This is a thunkgeofructor," said Arpelson.

"Don't expect me to munch on that," said Darcee, "it's not right to hit on a try zwei."

"Zwei bist du spracht Anglais le porcinesque," said Arpelson.

"You speak Slurian," said Darcee, "Toto never gets what I say."

"Well, as a lover of stumbled memories I must get a tongue de Slurian," said Arpelson.

"Oh, wow," said Darcee, "I… I… I think I love you, Arpelson of one name."

Arp furrowed his nose.

"Really?" he said in dubiousity and absolute delight.

Sixteen:
Darcee Klings
24th April 2020; 7:47PM

"I want to be with you all places, Arp, arp arp man. Like a singing tonal box of promises."

Arp laughed inwardly so much his face bunched up like a man 13 years his senior.

"Never been in love?" he said, kicking a schoon-pebble on the shore.

"Well, I had a fantasy pal," said Darce', "as a toddler."

"I am quite real," said Arp.

"Nice," said Darcee and reached for Arp's hand but caught herself, "sorry, Arp, I just have been bottled up."

"I know all about djinns," said Arp, "we be of a sort akin to one another and not to compulsion."

"One and one are infinity," said Darcee.

"Who taught you that?" wondered Arp. "It's curious and intriguing."

"First thing's first." said D.

Seventeen:
Eedgar's X
24th April 2020; 7:56PM

Eedgar Claasmouth was returning a knick-knack to Ludwig Othello.

"I don't enjoy it," he said, tawdry and vaccuous.

"Not my babessiue," said Mr Othello, "go and despite the warchinosophiopities."

Eighteen:
Maltiverse
24th April 2020; 8:04PM

Darcee was at Thanks Cafe giving a drink to Arp; it tallied up to $2.

"2 cents please," said Darcee, and poked out her tongue.

"Coda," said Arp, and blew a raspberry.

"Tale-man," said Darcee.

"I've said nothing," said Arp.

"I'm noting that," said Darc.

"O wow," said Arp, "what is this? Milkish? Protein weiz?"

"It's LoveMaltYouMetThatIDid." said Darcee. "That's a mouthful." said Arp.

Nineteen:
#MHM
24th April 2020; 8:07PM

Nanna Rosa was in her cell and she was listing goals on her fingers.

"I want to see Tabs and Darc'," she said, "I want Tobes to be a Dad, I want my son to spring me out, that's what I want."

She sat back on a harsh painted tar coloured bench of petrified wood in a cold, grey greasewater cell.

"Benmann," she prayed, "I see from my grandchildren that you somehow… *somehow* rule this world but why are there still bad things for an old Nan like me? Do you know? What's in deep heart yours?"

She sat back. Her phone hung on the hook with a white, curly cable leading to the grey banana like receiver that linked it to the azure box with tooth coloured number key-buttons.

Twenty:
Starwyrm Holds
24th April 2020; 8:17PM

The Starwyrm was talking in Gohm Toby's mind canvas.

"A lot of old stars that no one visits," it said, "I make them less dense, and then they don't need to eat so much, and I give that mass as a song to W.C. Benmann."

Twenty-One:
Mother Rosa^2
24th April 2020; 9:16PM

At the Rosa Folks: Mama Rosa ate a pecan pie; a small one, that Darcee had constructed with Toto's boss style foodie, as Mama Rosa approximated in her slangthink. "They are funny, my gals," she thought, "and this is cheap and crazy. I do enjoy this so much. Good on Darcee. And so on."

Twenty-Two:
Otbye
24th April 2020; 9:21PM

For all he knew, Ludwig O had a night to himself

"A, the lady, she ain't go' no' to t'me oop arp op." said Othello.

Anna Othello-Batt, Gohm Toby's mother, was listening to Lud' go on on his own and he ain't himself. That's what she thought.

Twenty-Three:
Codanthem
24th April 2020; 9:28PM

Eedgar Claasmouth played clavichord on the beach and sung a short Codanthem.

O.P.U.S.T.V.A.P.I

I ache and I do not lie

I go do so well you shy

I see to you be ki

And Toto with Gohm clapped.

Eedgar looked goadworthy and tried a shy bow of the brow.

Twenty-Four:
Toto's And Hare
24th April 2020; 9:37PM

Toto and Gohm saw Darcee and Arp making silly faces in the cafe. Toto made a silly face at Gohm and she got a really tight side-hug.

Twenty-Five:
Warden Detcod
24th April 2020; 9:39PM

At the Prison, Nanna Rosa was addressing security man Warden Detcod.

"Do you like work?" she asked.

"I keep you deep," Detcod said.

"Sometimes air is needed to rise up to go." said Nanna Rosa.

Twenty-Six:
Mister Rockabye
24th April 2020; 9:43PM

On Thanksome Beach, a collectible rock stood up.

"Love to be so woo," he said, "Come back Arp, we rocks miss all you be, bring Darcee, we can play rock games, will be so fun!"

And water wept cause he sung to self.

Twenty-Seven:
Foub Metamo'
24th April 2020; 9:47PM

Foub Fyrestead was busking in the Village Green to lil' kids.

"What do you like to hear?" he asked.

"Tell us facts," they said.

"I know the heart," said Foub.

"Is that a fact?" said a 4 year old.

Twenty-Eight:
The Humvoldt Mystery!?
24th April 2020; 9:55PM

Sylvia Humvoldt the stitchy, itty bitty doctor toy ate a raspberry for once in her life and she was amazed!

"You've got guts," said Othello.

"No worries," said Sylvia.

"dat's what Me feel when we are healed."

And that's a fact!

Twenty-Nine:
A.T.S.F.O.N^3
24th April 2020; 9:58PM

And Othello found a new chord. O#.

Thirty:
The Gorgon Star
24th April 2020; 10:00PM

In Othello's journal there had appeared a story between entries, as if by joy and dedication, it was the Gorgon Star story, a star with 27417.814 sides.

Thirty-One:
Motomotobototo's
24th April 2020; 10:07PM

"Guess what I call this dish?" cooed Darcee to her sister, all steam and joy and love and cheekiness.

"Something established," said Tot, and blundered a raspberry at her unmarried sister and laughed and flicked a fork of the stuff at Arp.

"That's how it starts," said Toby.

And Arp laughed.

Thirty-Two:
More Othello Chords
24th April 2020; 10:11PM

4^# #^2 M+^4 M+T

Thirty-Three:
Be Real
24th April 2020; 10:13PM

Let's give W.C. Benmann a HAND! Yay! Thanks for Thanks! Yay! Yay! Yay. Let Tabs say YAY! Let Tobes say YAY! EVEN NANNA ROSA! YAY!

Act 2:
To A Star, Toby Batiste

Thirty-Four:
Safe
28th April 2020; 7:45AM

Is this what you expected to happen next?

Nanna Rosa sat in her cell and a Starwyrm appeared toward her in a dream, and a burrow it had created formed a powderly path between… Thanks and the Prison.

"Thanks, is freedom," said Nanna and walked on through.

Thirty-Five:
Trophy
28th April 2020; 7:50AM

Arp and Darcee were eating honey buns by the beach when they discovered a Trophy, bright, gold with grey trim washed up on the beach with 3 barnacles on their lip.

"We won," cried Darcee, clapping her hands, "shall we race, knowing we won? Toto will be jello."

"Don't shake family," said Arp.

"We need to bless them, and help them to get their own prize."

Thirty-Six:
Good Lock
29th April 2020; 6:50AM

Tabula and Toby were resting in the village green.

"Psst," said Arp from across a tree.

"Hey," said Tabula, "Arp, what are you doing?"

"I need confession," said Arp, "to Toby."

"Me, what…" said Gohm.

"It's me, Luke Kuel." said Arp, "Tabula renamed me quite a little while ago."

"Tabs," cried Gohm, "Arp, we should have given a name as a team."

"In my heart you were with me," said Tabby and kissed Toby on the cheek.

"Darc', she hasn't twickenhamed on yet," said Arp, once Luke Kuel, "what to see to sigh, see?"

"She'll see," said Toby," maybe we can find a cube and she will see that you knew her when we were hosting our parties and smelling roses."

"O yeah!" said Arp, "Sylvia Humvoldt might know! Let's find her!"

Thirty-Seven:
Toto^2
29th April 2020; 7:08AM

Toto looked at her hands.

"I don't think I've been doing enough gardening with you, Gohm Toby."

"Well, we can pull weeds outside our house," said her spouse.

And as they were they discovered a solid clunk beneath trowels.

And there in the soil was a grey cube. And Toby and Toto held hands over it and nodded.

This… exactly what we need." said Tabula.

Thirty-Eight:
Orange Legion
29th April 2020; 7:14AM

They got to Darcee who was eating a melon. She had made a lot of clumsy bites with her small teeth.

"Lovely," said Tabs, "oof you."

She cuddled her sister, and placed the grey cube on Darcee's head.

And it unpacked into a cross and settled like a legionnaire's hat and Darcee laughed.

"Well," she said, "that is intense, what do you call it. A grey-square-matter?"

Thirty-Nine:
Mention Of Your Brain
29th April 2020; 7:20AM

"Well, Grey Square Matter," said Darcee to her cube hat, "shall we see just what you see, for I see all sides and you sway me to see what you saw."

And she saw weird.

"What do you mean weird," said Tabula.

"I mean stuff that's dammed up waiting to be revealed," said Darcee, "like I see days and seconds and hours and years and centuries."

"Historical feat," said Toby.

"Hey! Tabs gasped enthusiastically, "you could be a historian. You could teach about all the dates. A pure educator for the land with no-one. And that's a good-thing, an educator."

"And so is being a chef," said sister Darcee, "wow, a *teacher*!"

"How we grow," said Toto, "expanding in our knowledge and understanding."

Forty:
Sote Ari Y-H
29th April 2020; 7:35AM

And…

Too much wore on in the next day.

"Darcee," said Tabula, "you know something about me, don't you?"

"I see you're pregnant," said Darcee.

"Oh, dandel-ionospheres!" said Totes.

"Is it a boy or a girl?" asked Toby

Sylvester Ryan Rosa Toby

25th February 2020
5:54PM

    Sometimes; in love; one has to write what one has to say;
    And I say that things happened;
    They happened thus;
    I trust you understand;
    That after many walks;
    And many verse of feathers;
    And verbage in all kinds of weather;
    Me and Gohm became
    A mother and a father;
    He went about his duties;
    As a gardener and mayor;
    And I would stay at home;
    And when he returned he'd do my hair;
    And then we'd sit together;
    At the bottom of the stair;
    And we would talk for hours;
    Toby; young and full of care;
    I bear this little one for you, my Gohm;
    I bear this little hope for us to share;
    Would you see him in his crib;
    When I have bought him to the world?
    What would you rather?
    Someone like you?

Othniel Poole

Or would you like a girl?
And we would sit;
And sometimes we would eat;
And Toby would experiment with seed;
He'd plant the things I required to feed;
To get me the right things on which to dine;
And sometimes that suited my fine;
And sometimes I was sick;
And there were certain herbs sincere;
And though a cure they were promise;
That the Prince of Peace;
Would bring an eye of chords
Into the tummies;
And my Dad, the Bushranger;
Would sit and talk with me;
And he'd give me little things that he had woven
Rough and coarse;
With rough green twine and hair of horse;
And I would put them as my overcoat;
And in the winter that was great;
Because when pregnant, however nice you feel;
Nobody wants some ice across their keel;
And I felt fine; no matter what my shape;
If Gohm's a fruit from some sort of tree;
Let me be a kindred beside him upon our cluster
Of the grape;
And Mother Rosa at the Time;
Huddled round me, and my sister;
Darcee was as a servant;

As a devoted one of light;

And with so very little pain;

We got it right;

And we had joy

A new life in the middle of the night;

Sylvester Ryan

Rosa Toby

Purple hair with flecks of grey

And small scales like silverside

In the cradles east and west

Of collarbone

Yes, we all have our differences;

Everyone to his own variation;

But little Silly Reez;

You are so safe with Gohm and me

Forever you'll be safe with Gohm and me;

I love you so

My little silver freckle;

My dear, dear, sweet young son;

And yes you are my very first one;

I love you so

My little Vettie Raz;

And none will Toby let on past;

Unless they are someone so safe;

That no foot of theirs

Would tread this latest grape;

Let Benmann be your Counsellor

Your prince of peace when you are dry

And now his home, where we are

Is on Earth;
He has affiliation with the sky
Let villages raise this small lad;
And let him have the fun we had;
But without iniquity;
And let his eyes with every shade
Even UV; infra-red
And let sweet dreams of Debir;
Fill his divine head
Amen;
6:06PM
25th February 2020

The Gulf Of Neglect

February 25 2020

Peace

25th February 2020
6:28PM

    Elohim brings peace;

    Seeking a face;

    And yet you find grace;

    Yeshua brings something;

    You couldn't find on your own;

    Walking a way;

    A pedal on a cycle path;

    And all the people who do not know how to read;

    Yet analyse like crazy;

    Laugh behind their metatarsals;

    God bless their big toe;

    God bless their wedding ring finger;

    God bless their sense of humour;

    It makes the world go round;

    It's potential to be a square;

    We'll read the story;

    Put in a library;

    And when the internet's erased;

    And you know it really is merely a phase;

    I shall see you in that

    Collection

    Right there.

    25th February 2020

    6:30PM

We'd like to know if you enjoyed the book. Please consider leaving a review on the platform from which you purchased the book